CRACKED CLEATS

BILL SUMMERS

FULL SUN PRESS

Cracked Cleats

First Edition: March 2019

ISBN: 978-0-9998979-5-9

Cover Design and Interior Formatting: Streetlight Graphics

FULL SUN PRESS
Basking Ridge, New Jersey

www.billsummersbooks.com

CHAPTER 1

ROLL WITH THE THUNDER, OR FLY WITH THE FALCONS?

Max Miles slid off his bed and swung his foot into the tennis ball. Swung too hard. The ball flew up. It didn't hit the wall, it hit glass. Max heard the noise. He was afraid to look. When he did, he saw the crack in his window pane, bottom right corner. *At least I hit the corner.* Max thought fast. He grabbed a picture off his bookshelf and placed it in front of the crack.

Max flopped on his bed and squeezed his eyes shut. *This is crazy. I've changed my mind fifty times, and now I'm breaking windows.* Two soccer teams wanted Max, but he could choose only one. He loved the Thunder, his travel team in Chelsea, Pennsylvania. But now Max had an offer to join the Falcons, the best under-thirteen academy team in the state.

Max tried to drift off, but his phone dinged. He read a text from Wesley "Fivehead" Cannon, his best friend, neighbor, and Thunder teammate. *Hey pal, I know you're sweatin' your decision. Wanna knock a ball around?* Max tapped, *See ya on the Square.*

Max threw on his workout gear. He took the stairs two at a time, stepped out to his deck, and laced his boots. A light mist floated in the air. Max fished a ball from the bin and jogged to the Square, the mini soccer field in his backyard. He was nine touches into a left-footed juggle when he heard the gate rattle. Still juggling, Max looked up to see Fivehead stepping into the yard. Marching in behind him was every one of Max's Thunder teammates.

Max felt his heart hammer. Fivehead walked up and put an arm around him. "Dude, we just took a vote. It was sixteen-zero, you're staying on the Thunder."

"Hah!" Max snorted.

"What's so funny?" Fivehead snapped. "Your decision is made, you should be relieved."

"You're quite the comic, Fiver."

Max and Fivehead chose up sides for a pick-up game. Max was the only guy in cleats, the other boys wore sneakers. Playing on the damp lawn, the boys racked up more grass stains than goals. After the short game ended, Max watched his teammates trail out through the gate. *Man, I love those guys. I'm really gonna miss 'em.*

Max kicked off his boots and climbed on his trampoline. He bounced the ball on the rubber floor. As the ball reached its apex, Max sprang up and lashed a bicycle kick into the netting. He was about to launch into a second smash when he heard the gate swing open. Fivehead again, this time alone. Max jumped off and they sank into the grass. Fivehead tucked his long blond hair behind his ears. "So, Max, I figured it out. You stay with the Thunder one more season, then you can fly off with the Falcons."

Max grabbed a few blades of grass and tossed them in the breeze. "The Falcons want me now, Fiver. What if it's now or never?"

Fivehead tried another angle. "Think about this, Max. Thunder is powerful, it roars across the sky. Falcons? You wanna be some beady-eyed bird? I mean, thunder scares the white stuff out of a falcon."

Max chuckled. Suddenly, the rain fell harder. Fivehead stood. "I gotta go. Call me with the good news, deal?" Max said nothing, and Fivehead walked out.

Max got up, grabbed his boots, and jogged inside. Plodding up to his room, he thought about Fivehead's description of a falcon. "Beady-eyed bird." Max opened his computer and searched 'Falcon.' He read: *The peregrine falcon reaches over two hundred miles per hour during its hunting dive. That makes it the fastest member of the animal kingdom. Falcons have large eyes that help them survive in the wild. They can see at least one mile and keep track of three moving objects at one time.* Max's jaw flew open. *Wow, falcons have great speed and great eyes, perfect for soccer.* But then he read the next fact: *Only twenty percent of a falcon's high-speed dives end in a successful kill.* Max shook his head at that. *That's weird. They take a lot of shots, but four out of five miss the target.*

Max picked up a pen, opened his note pad, and drew a line down the center of the page. On one side he wrote his reasons to stay on the Thunder. On the other, he listed why he should join the Falcons. He counted, four to four. *I hate ties*. Max rolled onto his bed. *I could flip a coin, but it would probably stand up in my carpet.*

Then Max grabbed his pad and re-read his first reason to join the Falcons - *get away from Red*. Red Peters, Max's enemy ever since he moved to Chelsea last summer. First, Red schemed to keep Max off the Thunder. When that didn't work, Red quit the Thunder and joined their rival, the Lightning. Then Red hit Max with cheap shots in two games, and bullied him in school. Max picked up his pen and drew a line through Red's name. *If I join the Falcons, I'll never have to play against that loser again.*

Max blew out a sigh. *Okay, I've made my decision, I'm a Falcon.* But then his eyes swung to three photos pinned on his bulletin board. One showed Max and his teammates, clowning around by the Liberty Bell before their tournament in Philadelphia a month earlier. Another showed Max and Fivehead holding the trophy after winning that event. In the third shot, Max hugged his coach, Jack Pepper. Max dropped on his bed. *I'm doing it again…making a decision, and then unmaking it.*

That night, Max was last to the dinner table. An uncomfortable silence hung in the room, until it was broken by Max's older sister, Betsy. "So, time's running out, Max. You decide?"

Max steered his eyes away from his mom. "I'm staying with the Thunder."

Out of the corner of his eye, Max caught his mom's sour expression. She snapped, "I hope you're doing this for you, Max, and not for Fivehead and your other teammates."

Betsy piled on. "Max, you join the Falcons and you'd be surrounded by really good players. You wouldn't get double-teamed all the time."

"I thought about that," Max said. "But I love my teammates. I'm not gonna take a chance with a bunch of guys I don't know."

"Sometimes you take chances," Betsy shot back. "If it was me, I'd join the Falcons in a snap."

"But it's me, not you," Max fired back.

Mr. Miles put a hand on Max's shoulder. "I know it's a hard decision, Max. I'm proud of how you've weighed the pros and cons."

"Thanks, Dad, but now I gotta tell Coach Ball I'm not joining the Falcons. Guess I'll send him an email."

"No, you need to call him," Mr. Miles pushed back. "You owe him that."

Max dug his fingers into his forehead. "I'll be so nervous, Dad. Can you do it?"

"Nice try, Max," said his dad. "Just thank him and say you're comfortable on the Thunder."

Max excused himself and pushed away from the table.

"What about the rest of your steak?" his mom called out.

"Lost my appetite," Max called over his shoulder. He climbed the stairs and grabbed Coach Ball's card from his desk. His heart thumping on his chest, Max tapped in the number. Half way through the first ring, he ended the call. *Maybe I'm not ready to decide after all.*

Max paced across his gray carpet. His phone dinged, the name *Gary Ball* on the screen. For three rings Max stared at the phone, and then he answered.

"Max, it's Coach Ball, I think you called."

Max tried to speak, but the words got trapped in his throat. Finally, he said, "Uh, Coach Ball, thanks for the chance to join the Falcons. I'm really sorry, but I'm staying with the Thunder."

After a long pause, Coach Ball spoke. "I'm sorry to hear this, Max. I know you'd be a great fit on the Falcons."

Max felt his chest harden like a block of ice. He fumbled for words but came up empty. "Max, are you there?" Coach Ball asked. At last, Max found his voice. "It was a hard decision. But I really like my team."

"I understand," Coach Ball replied. "Hey, the Thunder and the Falcons both play in the Big Apple Tournament in New York City this May. Maybe I'll get to see you then. I hope you have a great season with the Thunder, Max."

"Thanks, Coach Ball." Max hung up. *Coach Ball sounds cool. Did I just screw up?*

A bit later, Max punched in Coach Pepper's number. Coach answered on the first ring. "Coach Pepper, it's Max. I'm staying with the Thunder."

"That's wonderful news, Max!" Coach blared. "Your teammates will be so pumped."

"Thanks, Coach," Max said. "I really sweated over this. But I got the best teammates, the best coach. I'd be crazy to leave."

"Yeah, especially since you're gonna be captain of the Thunder."

"Coach, did you say, 'captain?'"

"That's right, captain Max."

Max felt a bolt of excitement - and alarm. "Coach, you sure about that? I mean, last fall you picked different captains for each game."

"True, Max, but you've earned this role," Coach replied.

"But all the other boys have been on the team much longer than me."

"Doesn't matter," Coach shot back. "You're always positive and you play your tail off. The boys look up to you, Max. They see you as their leader."

Max didn't know what to say to that. Coach went on. "I'll announce it at our first indoor practice. We can meet up before then, go over what I expect."

A minute later Max clicked off, and then he popped Fivehead a quick text. *Staying with the Thunder.* The reply came in a flash. *Pump me up, bro!*

Two mornings later, Max was pouring syrup on his French toast when he heard the newspaper land on the porch. He went out and scooped up the *Chelsea Chimes*. A chilly gust nudged him back inside. Max sat and took out the sports section. The headline screamed at him.

RED PETERS PICKED FOR FALCONS SOCCER TEAM

CHAPTER 2

CAPTAIN MAX, ANGRY ARTIE

MAX'S JAW FELL OPEN. *No way!*

He read the story. *Red Peters has been chosen to play for the Falcons, a top academy soccer team for under-thirteen boys. Last fall, Peters was the leading scorer in the Chelsea travel league, with eighteen goals. "Red is a phenomenal athlete and a natural scorer," said Gary Ball, Falcons coach. "He's the best player I scouted."*

Max felt his heart pound. *Best player you scouted? What about me!* Max stared at the picture of Red next to the story. *That's the first time I've seen the kid smile.* Max ripped out the picture, balled it up, and dunked it in the trash bin. He sank back in his chair and ran his hands over his black bristles. *Why am I so ticked off? I should be dancing on the table – I don't have to play against that goon any more.*

But Max knew why he was angry. Red had joined an elite team. *Now people will think Red is better than me. That's crazy! The only reason he's on that team is because I turned down Coach Ball's offer. No way is that punk better than me, just ask my teammates!*

Max thumped his fist on the table. *Maybe I shoulda joined the Falcons. But it's too late, that chance has flown away.*

That Saturday, Max was dribbling a tennis ball across his bedroom carpet when his phone dinged, a text from Coach Pepper. *Max, meet at Mickey's Diner at noon?* Max tapped back, *See you there.*

Two hours later, Max set out on the four-block walk into town. Half way there, he looked up at dark clouds gathering. *This captain thing makes me nervous. Coach says my teammates respect me, but do all of them? I mean, I just joined the team a few months ago.*

Suddenly, Max could feel bits of moisture dot his face. Raindrops or snowflakes, he couldn't tell. But cold. The sleet fell harder, pushing Max into a jog until he reached Mickey's. Climbing the steps, Max passed a lady on a ladder, hanging a holiday wreath on the window. He stepped in and spotted Coach Pepper's white ball cap, with 'THUNDER' on the bill in bold black letters.

Max walked over, and Coach stood and hung an arm around him. They sat, and a minute later Max ordered lemonade and a grilled cheese sandwich. Coach asked for coffee and an omelet with ham and Swiss cheese. Coach leaned across the table and spoke in a low voice. "Okay, Max, tell me how this sounds... '*Now taking the field, Thunder captain, Max Miles.*'"

Max put up his hands. "I don't know, Coach. I mean, I'm still new. Everybody else has been on the team like, forever. Some other guys want to be captain, I'm sure."

Coach waved that off. "You work harder than anyone, Max. You stand up for your teammates. And you're the best dang twelve-year-old I've ever seen. So, in my eyes, you've earned this honor." Coach pulled a sheet of paper from his shirt pocket and set it in front of Max. "Here's what I look for in a captain. Let's go through it."

Max eyed the word at the top of the sheet – ACRONYM. "Coach, that first word, what language is that?"

Coach snorted. An English teacher at the middle school, he loved words. "ACK-ROW-NIM," Coach said. "It's a way to shorten a series of words. You take the first letter of each word in the phrase. You put them together, and, bang, you have an acronym."

Max put up his hands. "Lost me, Coach."

Coach nodded. "So, Max, what's your favorite TV channel?"

"ESPN," Max said.

"When the company was founded, do you know what ESPN stood for?" Coach asked.

Max thought for a second. "No idea."

"It stood for, 'Entertainment and Sports Programming Network.' That's a mouthful, right? So, ESPN was an acronym for the full name of the channel."

Max nodded. "Okay, now I get it."

A bit later the food came. Coach sliced up his omelet, shoveled in a forkful, and eyed Max. "Now look at the acronym on your list."

Max eyed 'CLEAT.' "Coach, cleat's a word, not an acronym."

"In this case, it's both," Coach explained. "Cleat is an acronym for the five things I look for in a captain. 'C' is for 'calm.' That means you keep your cool at all times."

"I'm good with that."

"It's going to be tougher this year, Max. Last fall, you snuck up on everyone. Now, everyone knows you. Opponents will be on you, like bees on honey."

"Bees on honey?"

"Think about it," Coach said. "Honey attracts bees, lots of bees. You're gonna be covered, like bees cover honey."

"Gee, that's great," Max cracked. "So, what about the 'L'?"

"That's for 'lead,' Coach explained. "Your teammates want to be like you. They will watch everything you do and hear everything you say. You lead, and they will follow."

Max could feel his heart beat a little faster. "How about the 'E'?" he asked.

Coach held up a big hand. "We're not done with 'lead' yet. As captain, I expect you to demand the best of your teammates. That means that sometimes, you'll have to get in their faces."

Max put up his hands. "Sorry, Coach, that's not me."

Coach fixed Max in a hard stare. "I never said being captain was easy, Max." Coach stuck in another hunk of omelet and went on. "Look, we have one player who likes to bark at teammates when they mess up."

"Would that be Artie?" Max guessed.

"Yep, and when Arties yaps, you need to put a leash on him."

Max took a bite of his sandwich. "If I give Artie lip, he'll go off like a firecracker."

"Don't sweat it, I'll help."

Coach eyed the sheet. "The 'E' stands for 'effort.' You push yourself, every minute you're on the field. That'll set a great example for your teammates."

Max saw an 'A' next.

"The 'A' is for 'attitude,'" Coach said. "Be positive, all the time."

"We have a good team, so there's no reason to be negative," Max said.

"We just got moved up to the top flight in the state," Coach volleyed. "We're not gonna win every game. When we lose, you need to be upbeat. Your attitude will rub off on everyone, trust me."

Max nodded. "What about the 'T'?"

"It stands for 'tough,'" Coach said. "You're gonna hear a lot of trash talk this year, Max. When opponents razz you, you gotta ignore it. Remember, your mouth is a weapon, but only when you don't use it." Coach popped in another piece of omelet, then pointed his fork at Max. "You're gonna get smacked around, too. Some guys will hit you with elbows, knees, and boots. You gotta take it like a man - and give it back, within the rules."

Max gritted his teeth. "Being captain sounds really hard. Maybe we should keep picking different captains for every game."

"You'll feel some pain, but pain makes you stronger," Coach replied. "I picked you, because I know you can handle some pain."

Max stared at the last bite of his sandwich. Finally, he stuck it in. A minute later, the waiter put the check on the table. As Coach took a few bills out of his wallet, Max heard the diner door swing open. He looked up, and suddenly that sandwich was doing back flips in his stomach.

There was Red Peters, walking toward him. He wore a black jacket with a gray falcon on the crest. Red looked at Coach Pepper, but said nothing. Then he faced Max. "Hey, Max, you like my jacket?"

"Cool falcon," Max answered.

Red shot Max a cocky smile. "So, I had my first practice with the Falcons yesterday. Team is wicked good."

"Good for you, Red," Max replied.

Red put his hands on the table and leaned in. "I can't wait for the Big Apple tournament in New York this May. We might even play against each other."

"That'd be cool," Max said.

Red snorted. "Yeah, cool for the Falcons. We'd win by ten goals."

Coach Pepper put money on the table and stood. "Ready to go, Max?"

Max got to his feet in a snap. "See ya around, Red." Red said nothing back. Max stepped past and followed Coach out the door. On the sidewalk, Coach gave Max a friendly jab on the arm. "You just had your first test as captain, and you nailed it. Red tried to ruffle you, but you kept calm. See, Max, you can do this."

Max said goodbye and took his first steps toward home. At the end of each stride, he heard his boots crush an inch of soft snow. *I love that sound, it's like the snow is saying, 'Ouch.'* Half way home, Max broke into a jog. *I'm captain of the Thunder, pretty neat. If I'd joined the Falcons, I'd never be captain.*

As Max reached Hickory Lane, he saw Fivehead playing with his poodle, Cocoa. The snow had turned the dog's fur from brown to white. "Fiver, I barely recognize Cocoa," Max called out. Fivehead chuckled as he jogged over to Max. "It's funny, I think Cocoa looks better with white fur. I might have to get some spray paint."

Max laughed. Fivehead asked, "So Max, you went into town without me?"

"I just met with Coach Pepper," Max said. "He wants me to be captain."

Fivehead broke into a grin. "Dude, that's great!"

Max swung his boot into the snow. "Artie will be ticked, you know it."

"Don't sweat Artie, Max. Coach will swat him like a gnat. Plus, all the guys like you, nobody likes Artie."

A few days later, Max walked into the gym at Chelsea Middle School for the Thunder's first winter practice. His pulse was bouncing, and when he saw Artie, it bounced even faster. As he loosened up a bit later, Max had a chat with himself. *Maybe I should tell Coach I don't want to be captain...nah, that would be wimpy...I can't let Artie Moss take me down.*

Coach Pepper blew his whistle, and the boys gathered. "Get ready for an exciting spring season, boys," Coach began. "We move up to a tougher league. And in May, we travel to New York City for the Big Apple tournament."

"Big apple, baby!" Fivehead blurted. "I'm pumped to the core!"

"Wesley, you're a nut," Coach said. He let a few seconds pass. Then he let his eyes rest on Max, and Max knew what was coming next. "I have some important news to share," Coach went on. "Our captain for the spring season will be Max Miles."

Max glanced at Artie. His lips were pinched shut, his arms crossed. "So, Coach, what happened to picking captains for every game?" Artie asked.

"Max has earned this," Coach replied.

"Says who?" Artie snapped. "He just joined the team. What about the guys who have been here since like, forever?"

Max felt a chill shoot down his back. Coach faced Artie. "Artie, we have lots of players who could be good captains. Truth is, Max has emerged as our leader. Everyone looks up to him."

Artie stood his ground. "Why don't you let the players pick the captain?"

"We'd all pick Max," Fivehead shot in.

"You're wrong," Artie sniped back.

Coach put up his hands. "Boys, Max is our captain, game over." He looked at Max. "Lead the boys on a few laps around the gym."

Max broke into a trot, the boys falling in behind him. Fivehead jogged up to Max. "Artie is really ticked," Max said.

"Sure is," Fivehead agreed. "If he was captain, he'd think he could bark at us like a hungry dog."

Max bit back a laugh. But what happened ten minutes later wasn't so funny. Early in a scrimmage, Fivehead flubbed a clearance and Ben drilled the free ball into the net.

"You can't give it away, Fiver!" Artie snapped. "Wake up!"

Max felt his heart race. *Do I say something?*

Now Fivehead and Artie had come face to face. "I don't need your crap, Artie," Fivehead shot back. As the boys glared at each other, Max felt his chest hammer. Finally, Coach Pepper stepped between the boys. His eyes fixed on Artie's, he said, "We don't criticize teammates for physical errors, Artie, got it?"

"But –"

"No buts, that's it!"

Coach backed away, and Max knew it. *I just had my first test with Artie, and I flunked.*

After practice, Coach asked Max to stay behind. The other players walked out, and then Coach set his eyes on Max. "Captain Max got tested pretty quick."

Max frowned. "I shoulda said something to Artie, sorry."

"Don't sweat it, I'll give you a pass today," Coach said. "But here's the deal. When Artie yells at a teammate for the wrong reason, you've got to get on him."

"What do you mean by the wrong reason?" Max asked.

"If Artie badgers a player for lack of hustle or a mental mistake, that's okay," Coach said. "But if he reacts to a physical error, like he did today, we can't have that. No guy who mis-hits a ball needs to be told he messed up. Got it?"

"He'll yap right back."

"Don't worry," Coach said. "I'll put a collar on him."

Max nodded.

As the spring season neared, Max felt better about his decision to stay with the Thunder. He never saw Red, because Red had transferred to a private school. None of Max's teammates were friends with Red, so he never had to hear about Red. But he did have to *read* about him. The weekend before the Thunder's first game in April, a headline in the *Chelsea Chimes* caught Max's eye.

PETERS LEADS FALCONS TO TITLE IN MARYLAND

Max read the first sentence. *Chelsea resident Red Peters scored two goals to lead the Falcons to a 3-2 win over a team from Holland in the championship match of an international soccer tournament held in Baltimore this weekend.*

Max looked at the photo below the story. It showed Red, getting mobbed by his teammates after his game-winning goal. Max gritted his teeth. *Okay, Red, it's game on. Next week, you get to read about my hat trick.*

CHAPTER 3

MAX ATTACKS

MAX WOKE ON SATURDAY THINKING about the dream he had just finished. He had dribbled a soccer ball across the whole state of Pennsylvania. He had pushed the ball between long rows of cornstalks, zigzagged through forests, even chugged up and over high hills. Sitting up, Max saw his blanket bunched at the end of his bed. *Wow, I kicked my blanket into a heap. Guess I made it to the Ohio border.*

Max rolled up his window shade and looked up at a few small clouds scattered across blue sky. He swung out of bed, flicked up the tennis ball, and juggled with his feet and thighs. On his thirteenth touch, the ball caromed off his foot and hit the carpet. *Thirteen's an unlucky number, can't stop on that.* He flicked the ball up and juggled to eleven before the ball spilled into the carpet.

Hearing the rattle of pans, Max scooted downstairs. He found his dad in the kitchen, making pancake batter. "I need an extra pancake today, Dad," Max said. "Feel a hat trick comin' on."

Mr. Miles spooned batter into a pan. "Max, you never talk about scoring. What's gotten into you?"

"I got a little competition going against Red Peters, Dad. I gotta outscore him, prove I'm better than he is."

Mr. Miles looked over his glasses at Max. "Did you and Red make a deal, or is this just in your head?"

"It's just me."

Mr. Miles pointed the spatula at Max. "Red Peters is out of your life, Max. You need to forget about him, now."

"How can I forget about him when I keep seeing his goofy face all over the paper?" Max griped.

Mr. Miles slid a strawberry pancake in front of Max. "Look, if you worry about scoring, it'll throw off your game. Just play to win, Max."

Max cut his pancake into eight pieces and dribbled out a pool of cinnamon syrup. *We'll win alright, with my three goals.*

Two hours later, Max led the Thunder onto the pitch for their opening match against the Sharks. As the game started, a strong wind blew in favor of the Sharks. Five minutes in, a Shark wing broke free near the corner and thumped a high cross. Theo came out, but the wind kicked up and swept the ball over his hands. The ball struck the back post and caromed into the net. His head hung, Theo retrieved the ball. As he turned out of the goal, Artie met him. "You messed up, Theo!" Artie snapped. "Play the wind!"

Max ran up. "Lay off, Artie, that wind is crazy."

"He shoulda had that ball, Max, and you know it!" Artie fired back, and then he jogged off. Max put a hand on his chest, felt his heart hammering.

For the rest of the half, the wind was like a twelfth player for the Sharks. Late in the half, a Shark wing cracked a cross that knuckled into the box. Artie misjudged the ball's speed. He leaped too late. The ball skimmed the top of his head and sailed behind him, right into the path of an unmarked Shark wing. The wing ran on, chested the ball down, and drilled a bolt past Theo into the far corner.

Max jogged to Artie. "It's the wind, Artie, forget about it." Artie nodded. Max ran off. *At least I got a nod out of him.*

At halftime the Thunder jogged off down by two. In the stands, Mrs. Miles wrung her hands. "The Thunder has no pop, they're gonna lose."

Betsy smirked. "Like you always tell me, Mom, keep your chin up. They got the wind in the second half. Besides, did you see Max's face as he jogged off? His eyes are on fire, and that means the Sharks are in big trouble."

The Thunder gathered around Coach Pepper, all eyes on the ground. "Pick your heads up, boys," Coach said. "Look, the wind changes uniforms in the second half." Coach checked his clipboard. "We're gonna make a change. Max will move up to left wing. Let's play balls down that side. Max can use his speed to create havoc."

"Havoc?" Fivehead echoed.

"It means he'll cause problems," Coach explained.

Early in the second half, Max did just that. In the circle, he swooped in on a foe and stripped the ball clean. His head up, Max dinked to Fivehead and took off. Fivehead chipped the ball ahead of Max. Max beat the center back to it and surged alone into the box. Max saw the keeper charging at him. He cocked his leg, dropping the keeper into a slide. Slowing his shooting leg, Max nudged the ball around the keeper. He caught up with it two yards from the end line, his angle tight. Using the side of his foot, Max nudged the ball toward the open net. He watched it roll past the near post, peck the far post, and bounce in. Max raced over and leaped into Fivehead's arms. "Great pass, Fiver!"

Minutes later, Ben plucked the ball from a thicket of legs in the circle and sprang free. Max accelerated down the line, and Ben lofted the ball into his path. Max gathered, but three opponents penned him in. His eyes up, he spotted Fivehead racing toward the far post. Max thumped a high cross ahead of Fivehead, who ran on and crushed a volley with his right boot. The ball sizzled past the keeper and stabbed the net in the far corner. Thunder 2, Sharks 2.

Now the Thunder had seized control. The wind blew even harder, knocking down every high ball off a Shark boot. The Thunder attacked like waves rolling onto the sand. First, Max rattled the post from twenty yards, and then Artie jarred the bar from ten. Two close calls, but still a tie game. When the Thunder earned a corner kick, Max ran to Fivehead. "I'll fake to the near post, circle back to the far post." Fivehead nodded.

As Fivehead lined up his kick, Max jogged toward the near post, but then he spun away from his mark. He turned to see Fivehead's cross, curling in ten yards off the goal line. Max figured the breeze would carry the ball closer to the goal. He jockeyed inside a defender, jumped, and nodded the ball down. It slipped under the keeper's left hand and bounced into the net. Thunder 3, Sharks 2.

Max jabbed a fist at the sky. He looked at his dad on the sideline. Mr. Miles held up five fingers. Max nodded. *Five minutes to get my hat trick.* When the Sharks got a corner, they pushed ten players into the box. Their left wing curled his kick toward the penalty spot, but Artie rose up and headed it clear.

Max broke for the ball. He beat two defenders to it and sped into the circle. Looking up, he saw only the Sharks' keeper, charging at him. The keeper tried to grab Max's shirt, but Max sidestepped him. Out of the corner of his eye, Max could see opponents closing in. He looked at the open goal forty yards away. *Here it goes.*

Max swept his right instep into the ball and collapsed to the grass. From his knees, he watched the ball sail toward the goal, the wind pushing it higher and farther. *Get down, ball, get down!* The ball nicked the bottom of the bar and brushed the net. Max rolled onto his back, and his teammates buried him. A minute later the ref blew the final whistle on a 4-2 Thunder win.

Coach called in the team. "My word for the day is 'COURAGE.' It means showing strength when you're up against a wall, and that's what you did today."

A bit later the huddle broke, and Max stepped over to his bag. Coach grabbed his arm. "You played great today, Max. I also saw you ball out Artie after he tore into Theo. That's what I expect out of my captain."

Max nodded. He didn't have the energy to speak. He trudged over to his family. His mom hugged him. "Max, you were phenomenal," she raved.

"Thanks, Mom."

Mr. Miles wrapped an arm around Max. "You were in motion the whole second half. I kept waiting for you to catch your breath, but you never did. I don't know how you do it, Max."

"My legs are sore, first time they've ever felt like this."

"You ran like you had a motor on your back," Betsy added. "I got tired watching you."

Max snorted at that.

Mrs. Miles took off her ball cap and flipped it to Max. "What's that for?" Max asked.

"I'm celebrating your hat trick, Max."

Later that night, Max was sprawled on the couch. The family was half way through a movie, but Max knew he wouldn't make the end. He stood. "I can barely keep my eyes open, gonna go to bed."

As he plodded up the stairs, Max could still

feel the ache in his calves. *What's goin' on with my legs? I mean, I thought I was in good shape.* In bed a few minutes later, Max started to replay his goals. He remembered his first two, but then he conked out.

The next day, Max got on his computer and checked the league website. When he saw that he was the only player to score three goals in the first game, he pumped his fist. But then it hit him. *Red's name won't be on here anymore, weird. I bet he still sends me those nasty emails.* A bit later his phone beeped, and Max opened an email. *I heard you smashed in three goals in your opener, Max. I'm very impressed, keep it rolling – Coach Gary.* Max read the message twice. *That's wild. I turned down Coach Gary, but he still has an eye on me.*

Max took the stairs to the kitchen. Betsy looked up from the *Chelsea Chimes*. "So, Max, here's a quote from the Sharks' coach. '*We had no answer for Max Miles. He ran us into the ground.*'"

Max flashed a smile. "I love it."

"Yeah, but everybody reads the Chelsea

Chimes, Max. You know what that means - you're gonna be a marked man."

"I'm cool with that," Max said. "You watch, I'm gonna get in the best shape ever. I'll be able to outrun anybody."

CHAPTER 4

MASHED MAX

In science class that Friday, Miss Pickett was leading a discussion when Max fell into a daydream. He was about to curl a free kick around a wall when he heard his name called. Max snapped out of his dream. "Uh, sorry Miss Pickett, did you ask me something?"

The room erupted in a volley of laughter. Miss Pickett glared at Max. "I asked if you were paying attention, Max. Now we know the answer." More snickers. Miss Pickett held her stare. "Keep your head in the room, Max, got it?"

"I will," Max said, his ears tingling with shame. *This is crazy, it's like soccer has invaded my brain.*

On Saturday morning, Max was jarred

awake by a *tat-tat-tat* noise in his backyard. He pulled back his curtain and saw a woodpecker hammering its beak into a tall oak tree. Max smiled. *Today I'm gonna play like that woodpecker, never let up.*

Two hours later at Liberty Park, Max was running a warm-up lap when he noticed two boys on the Rampage, twins, pointing at him. Tall and wiry, both boys wore their stringy black hair down on their shoulders. Max looked away for a bit, then looked back. Four eyes, still on him. *What's up with that?*

Max opened the match by tapping to Ben and swinging out to the flank. Sensing two shadows in his midst, Max curled back across the pitch, his finger pointing at the grass in front of him. Ben tried to feed him, but one of the twins stepped in and blasted the ball away.

As the game unfolded, Max tried hard to shake off the twins. But they boxed him in with physical play, a shoulder here, a quick shirt tug there. In the stands, Betsy turned to her mom. "Max is working hard, but he's barely sniffed the ball."

"He's getting knocked around," Mrs. Miles griped. "The ref needs to blow his darn whistle."

When one twin broke up another pass meant for Max, he swept his boot through the grass. *There's only one way I'm gonna get the ball. It's time to roam.* As the Rampage swung the ball around the back line, Max set his sights on the left back. The back took control of a pass, and Max charged at him. The boy tried to make a lateral pass, but Max had read his eyes. He lunged and got his boot on the ball. Building speed toward the box, Max could hear his foe breathing over his shoulder. Max cocked his leg to shoot, but the boy slid in and chopped him down. Needles of pain stabbed Max's hip, but he scrambled up and shook it off.

The ref whistled a foul, but Max wanted more. "Come on, ref, book that kid!" Max screeched.

The ref ignored Max and jogged off. Max brushed a clump of dirt off his shorts and jogged toward the box for Fivehead's free kick. As he settled in near the penalty spot, one of the twins grabbed his shirt. Max locked eyes with the boy and blurted, "I don't grab your hair, why do you grab my shirt?" A second later, Fivehead's kick sailed past Max and bounced over the end line.

"Max!" Coach Pepper hollered. Max looked to the sideline, and saw Coach tapping a finger to his head. A spark of anger ran through Max. *That was stupid, gotta keep my cool.* The half ended scoreless. Max had not taken a single shot. He had drawn six fouls, but the Thunder had nothing to show for it.

The boys gathered at the bench. Coach Pepper paced, his big arms crossed. "Look, they got at least two guys on Max, on him like extra shirts. That means we have open players! Keep your eyes up. Hit the open man, and move off your pass to be a target. That's how we win this game."

"I'll work harder, try to get open more," Max followed.

After the huddle broke, Coach pulled Max aside. "I'm worried about you, Max. You've been running like a river, and your face is pale. Maybe you should sit for a while."

"No way, Coach. I'm good to go."

Coach paused for a beat. "Okay, but catch your breath between runs, got it?"

"Got it."

When the second half began, Max kept making bold runs. But each time he got the ball, the Rampage built a fence around him. Max passed well out of traps, but his teammates failed to muster any potent chances. After the Rampage keeper hauled in a high cross, Max looked over at his dad. Peace sign. *Two minutes left, time to put my mark on this match.*

Max settled under the keeper's punt and killed it on his thigh. Seeing Ben shoot up the flank, Max chipped toward the corner. As Ben gathered, Max scampered for the box. One twin tried to grab his shirttail, but Max wriggled free. Ben's cross came sweeping in, and Max studied the ball's flight. *It's a perfect angle, time for a bicycle kick.*

Crossing the eighteen, Max turned his back to the goal and leaped. He swung his left leg up and lashed his right boot at the ball. Max knew from the meaty *'thunk'* of boot on ball that it was a clean strike. As he crashed to the turf, he turned and saw the ball rise over the keeper. *Bonk!* The ball rattled the bar and plopped into the goalmouth. An alert Ben got to the bouncing ball first. In his excitement, he swung too hard and spooned it over the top.

"Ben, come on!" Artie shrieked.

Max sprang up and ran to Artie. "I told ya, Artie, don't yell at your teammates."

Artie locked eyes with Max. "He just blew a tap-in, Max."

Max was about to respond, but Ben beat him to it. "Artie's right, Max. I screwed that up, big time."

Max looked at Ben. Artie had jogged away. Max gnashed his teeth. *I hate being captain.*

The game ended in a scoreless deadlock. After the Thunder shook hands with the Rampage, Coach called the boys in. "My word for the day is 'REDOUBLE,'" he said. "It means to increase your effort when you're up against it." Coach rubbed his hands on his cheeks. "Look, Max was surrounded the whole game. When that happens, you all need to redouble your effort."

A bit later Max reached the car. "Worst game of my life," he whined. "I hardly ever got the ball."

"Those twins really hounded you," his mom said.

"Yeah, they were pretty cagey. They hit me with a bunch of cheap shots, but only when the ref wasn't looking. The refs better wake up, or I'll start going after guys."

"You can't do that, Max," his dad volleyed.

"Wanna bet?" Max countered.

They got in the car. Mrs. Miles looked at her note pad. "You took only two shots, Max."

Max tossed his head back. "Thanks for rubbing it in, Mom. I tried, you know."

Mr. Miles struck a positive note. "Your bicycle kick was spectacular, Max."

"Yeah, three inches too high."

"Ben really blew that rebound," Betsy piped in.

Max shook his head. *Betsy sounds like Artie, but she's right.*

When they got home, Max got out and stepped toward the backyard. "Where are you going?" his dad asked.

"I got work to do," Max replied.

Mr. Miles shot him a look. "You just chugged like a cheetah for eighty minutes. That's enough for one day."

But Max kept going. Over the next thirty minutes, he ran through some dribbling drills and cracked a bunch of shots with each foot. At last, he climbed on the trampoline and whacked ten bicycle kicks into the netting. After the last one, Max sank to the soft rubber floor and closed his eyes. *I got double-teamed the whole game. That stinks.*

The next morning, Max slept late. He got up, sank to his carpet, and stretched his legs. Feeling loose, he tapped a text to Fivehead. *Gonna take an easy jog – wanna join?*

Fivehead's reply was quick. *You're nuts. I'll look for ya on my bike.*

Max popped out the front door, clicked his watch, and stepped into a jog. It was a humid morning, the air thick. After ten minutes, Max felt beads of sweat trickle into his brow. As he reached the halfway point at the bottom of Hickory Lane, his watch read 12:30. He thumped his chest. *Too slow.* Max ran faster. As he started his third mile, he felt a cramp in his leg but ignored it. Finally, he could see his mailbox a hundred yards ahead, and he broke into a full sprint. Passing his mailbox, Max stopped his watch and threw himself onto his lawn. He checked his watch. 23:58. *Beat my goal by two seconds!* He began to stretch. *I'm gonna be so fit, no kid will be able to stay with me.*

At the end of practice on Tuesday, the boys huddled around Coach Pepper. He dug into his backpack and took out a folder. "Our Big Apple tournament is coming up. It's time we learn some cool things about New York City."

"Come on, we already know about New York," Fivehead whined. "It's big and dirty, and the streets are clogged with yellow cabs."

Coach fixed Fivehead in a playful stare. "That's great, Wesley, but now it's time you learn something useful."

Fivehead shook his head. "Nice try, Coach, but you know I'm allergic to learning."

The boys hooted. Coach held up the folder. "Each sheet in here lists a famous place in New York City, and a job that goes with it. I want you to write a story on the place and the job, three hundred words."

Fivehead groaned. "Three hundred words? That's like a book."

"Piece of cake, Wesley," Coach answered.

But Ben wagged a finger. "Coach, you

haven't seen Fiver write. When he picks up a pen, his hand starts to shake."

The boys roared. Coach called Max up first, and Max eyed his sheet. *Museum of Natural History, paleontologist.* Max looked at Coach. "Coach, I get the museum, but paleo-what?"

Coach grunted. "Do a little research, Max, you'll figure it out."

Ben was next. *Statue of Liberty, architect.*

Fivehead took the third sheet. *Central Park, hot dog vendor.*

Fivehead gave Coach the eye. "So, Coach, you sayin' I'm gonna be a hot dog vendor?"

Coach smiled. "Wait till you see how many hot dogs they sell, Wesley. I bet you would relish that job."

Fivehead smiled back. "That's a good one, Coach, for a weenie."

Coach lunged at Fivehead, but he darted away. Each player took an assignment. "I want you to dig deep," he said. "Visit the library. Do searches on the Internet. On the bus to New York, we'll share what we learned."

"Hang on, Coach, you forgot one person," Fivehead said.

Coach shot Fivehead a puzzled look. "Everybody got a sheet, right?"

"Everybody but you," Fivehead snapped.

Coach shook his head. "Don't worry, Wesley, I'm doin' my homework. I'll share some fun facts about New York."

Coach went back to his clipboard one more time. "Our hotel in New York sits only two blocks from Central Park," he said. "We'll get to know the park well, because we play our games there. Plus, we'll have enough free time to visit two places."

"Empire State Building!" Fivehead blurted.

"Intrepid Sea, Air and Space Museum," Ben followed.

"Yankee Stadium," Artie called out.

"Hang on, boys." Coach held up another stack of papers. "I've listed six cool places on this sheet. Decide what places you want to visit. Put a 'one' next to your top pick, and a 'two' next to your second pick. Give me your sheet at practice next week. We'll visit the two places most of you want to see."

Max took a sheet and eyed the list. *Wow, this trip will be a blast, even if I have to be a paleo-whatever.*

After school on Wednesday, Max tore through his homework. Looking out on the Square, he saw the sun lighting up the grass. He changed, stretched, shuffled downstairs, and stepped out the door. *It's a perfect day to run. Time to bang out three miles, beat twenty-three minutes.*

Along the route, Max knew each mailbox that marked off each mile. As he passed the yellow mailbox one mile out, his watch read 8:10. *You're waddling like a penguin, Max.* He clicked into a higher gear, and after two miles his watch read 15:40. *Better, but I still gotta pick up my pace.* Sweat dribbling into his eyes, Max sprang into longer strides. Finally, he reached the last turn in the road, and he could see his mailbox in the distance. Over the last twenty yards, Max burst into a sprint. Crossing his mailbox, he checked the numbers. 22:59.

Max pumped a fist and spilled into the grass. His eyes closed, he felt the warm sun on his face. Then, the ping of a bike bell jolted him. Max looked up to see Fivehead rolling to a stop. "Don't tell me you went for another run," Fivehead snapped.

"Yup, three miles."

Fivehead shook his head. "Dude, you're crazy."

"Come on Fiver, I got two guys on me all the time. If I want to see the ball, I gotta be able to run forever."

"Maybe, but I still think you're crazy. Hey, I'm ridin' to Mort's for a cone. Wanna come?"

"No more ice cream until we win a game, Fiver."

Fivehead threw his head back. "Okay, now I *know* you're crazy."

Fivehead pedaled off. Max clambered up and went into the garage. He drained a bottle of water, grabbed a second bottle, and headed for the backyard. Max toed the chalk and bolted thirty yards across the Square. Seven more times he raced from line to line. His shirt soaked through, he went inside and flopped on the couch. *This is awesome, I've never been in better shape.*

On Thursday, Max lashed in three goals during the scrimmage at practice. After school on Friday, he set out for a short run, to the yellow mailbox and back. But when he reached the mailbox, a little man is his head told him to keep going. A bit later Max passed his mailbox, another three-mile run in the books. He walked out back and dropped into the thick grass in the Square. *Can't wait for tomorrow, gonna jump the Jaguars.*

CHAPTER 5

RED IN THE FACE

FIVE MINUTES INTO DINNER THAT night, Max hadn't spoken a word.

"You're awfully quiet, Max," his dad said.

"Thinking about my game tomorrow," Max answered.

"Did I see you finishing a jog this afternoon?" his mom asked.

"Just a quick one."

"How quick?" his dad asked.

"Three miles."

"That's too much the day before a game, Max," his dad fired back. "What's gotten into you?"

Max stabbed at a pea. It took him three times to spear it. "I got two guys on me. If I stand still, they grab my shirt, and the ref never calls it. My only chance is to outrun 'em."

Mrs. Miles jumped in. "You're not a machine, Max. You're pushing yourself way too hard."

Max tossed his head back. "You said it yourself, Mom. I'm not getting the ball, not getting any shots. I gotta do more."

Now it was Betsy's turn. "You never stand still, Max. This is on your teammates. They need to get you the ball."

Max stared at the ceiling. *This is great. On the field, I get double-teamed. At dinner, I get triple-teamed.* He stuck his fork in a crouton, and it broke in half.

After dinner, Max went up to his desk. He got out his assignment notebook and flipped to the 'soccer' page. *Write three hundred words on the Museum of Natural History, paleontologist.* Max counted the syllables in paleontologist. *Six, that's three over my limit.* He did a search on 'Museum of Natural History' and up popped a photo showing the skeleton of a huge dinosaur. Max read the caption. 'A paleontologist discovered this skeleton over a hundred years ago in Wyoming.' Max nodded. *Hey, this paleo-thing might be cool after all.*

Max read for a bit and jotted some notes, but then his eyes started to close. He stood and tumbled onto his comforter.

At Liberty Park the next morning, Coach Pepper paced in front of the bench. "We're making a change," he said. "Max will move to center back, Artie will move up to center mid. This way, Max can sneak up into the attack, catch the Jaguars by surprise."

Artie scratched his cleats in the turf. "I don't like it," he whined.

"We need to shake things up, Artie," Coach shot back.

"Come on, I haven't played midfield in years," Artie retorted.

"It's worth a try, Artie," Max cut in. "I'll get ya the ball, for sure."

"It's a big risk," Artie fired back.

"When you're in a rut, you have to take risks," Coach said. "Let's make it work."

In the third minute, Fivehead made a clean tackle and spooned the ball down the flank. As Ben ran the ball down, Max raced across the center stripe and darted toward the box. Ben crossed, and a Jaguar headed the ball right into Max's path twenty yards from goal. As Max neared the ball, he sensed two Jaguars closing in. He beat the first foe, but the center back made a clean tackle and cracked the ball up the flank. Max sprang up, and he and the back locked eyes. "You're so overrated, boy," snapped the back, Kenny King. "Max Miles, huh? You should change your name to Max Inches."

Max felt his pulse spike up. "Shut your mouth, punk."

Max jogged off. *Come on Max, why did you waste words on that punk?* A bit later Max cut off a Jaguar cross and dribbled free out of the box. Fivehead bolted toward the far corner, and Max bashed a long ball ahead of him. As Fivehead chased it down, Max barreled toward the box. Fivehead collected near the corner and cracked a powerful cross. The keeper ran out and punched the ball, straight into Max's path.

Max took the bouncing ball off his chest and let it drop. Three Jaguars closed in. To his right, Max saw Fivehead cut into the box. He dinked a roller into Fivehead's path. Fivehead dribbled once and shot from fifteen yards, but the ball rose over the bar.

"Fiver!" Max yelped. But then he caught himself. "Good try, buddy, you'll get the next one." Max jogged away. *Come on, Max, you sound like Artie. Shut it!*

A bit later, Theo punched out a cross. Max ran onto the ball and pushed it into open space. As he dribbled into the circle, he let the ball get too far ahead. Kenny King stepped up and made a crunching tackle. On his follow-through, Kenny's boot caught Max below the shin guard. "Ahhh!" Max wailed as he crumpled to the grass.

The ref waved play on. Kenny surged forward into open space. He dribbled to the arc, snaked around Artie, and lashed a rocket toward the far corner. Theo dove. The ball sailed over his hands, struck the post, and settled in the net. Jaguars 1, Thunder 0.

Max hobbled to the ref. "Come on, ref, I got kicked!"

The ref ignored him.

In the stands, Mrs. Miles turned to Betsy. "Max is really amped up."

Betsy nodded. "I hope he doesn't explode."

Max started to jog back to his spot, but his

ankle throbbed. He waved at Coach Pepper and hobbled toward the bench.

"Where'd he get you?" Coach asked.

"My shin, it's pounding."

Coach fetched an ice pack from the cooler and tossed it to Max. He sat and held the pack to his shin. A minute later the half time whistle blew. Coach faced Max. "How's your leg?"

Max didn't move. "Not bad."

"You didn't get up," Coach said. "That means you're done for the day."

Max sprang off the bench. "No way, I'm going back in."

"Don't argue with me," Coach shot back. "Take a seat."

Max fired his water bottle into the grass and slumped on the wood.

With seven minutes to play, Kenny King thumped a rocket into the corner from long range to give the Jaguars a two-goal edge. As Kenny jogged back to his side, he looked over and threw Max a taunting smile. Max spiked the ice bag into the grass, stood, and took a few strides. His shin hurt, but not enough. He approached Coach Pepper. "My leg's fine, I gotta play."

Coach looked Max in the eye. "Lemme see you run."

Max ran off, turned, and darted back.

"How much pain?"

"None."

Coach let a few beats pass. "I'll put you in, but you better keep your cool, got it?"

"I got it."

A minute later, Max ran on at midfield. His shin hurt, but he did his best to block it out. Two minutes later, Max pounced on a loose ball near the circle. His adrenaline pumping, he sidestepped one foe, build speed, and carved a path around two Rampage backs.

As Kenny King swung over, Max eyed Ben free to his right. He faked a shot, drawing Kenny into a lunge. Slowing his downswing, Max slid the ball into Ben's path. Ben ran on and hammered a low bolt that snuck inside the far post. Rampage 2, Thunder 1.

Max and Kenny locked eyes. Max gave him a slight nod, and then he jumped into the swarm around Ben. As Max started back to his side, he noticed the Rampage coach huddled with two of his players. *Here we go again.*

Max was right. Suddenly, he had two

shadows following his every move. When the Rampage won a throw-in near midfield, Max looked over and saw his dad raise three fingers. *Do it now, Max.*

The thrower tossed up the line. The ball squirted out of a forest of legs, and Max latched on and took off. He blew past two players in the circle and tore into free space up the opposite flank. Suddenly alone, Max began to cut in toward the box. His eyes up, he saw Kenny King edging over. Max faked a shot, pushed the ball wide of Kenny, tapped once more, and cocked his leg. As Max met the ball, Kenny slid in. He got a boot on the ball and clipped Max to the turf.

As the balled rolled out of play, Max and Kenny scrambled up, face to face. "Told ya, boy, you're all hype," Kenny snapped. Max looked at the ref. "This kid mouths off a lot, card him." The ref ignored Max.

As the clock ticked down, Max was bottled up. But then he saw Kenny steal a pass in the circle and dribble into the Thunder half. *That punk got my shin, it's time to even the score*. Max ran up, slid, and tried to hook the ball off Kenny's foot. He was too late. He caught Kenny's heel, and Kenny tumbled face-first onto the ball.

The whistle blew. The ref ran up to Max. A vein bulged in his neck. Max felt his chest pound. *I'm gonna get a card.*

He was right. The ref held a card over Max's head. The card was red.

Max sank to his knees. "You can't give me a red card!"

"That was a reckless tackle from behind. Now get up and get off!"

Max trotted slowly to the bench. Artie ran over. "Nice job, captain."

This time, Max had nothing to say back. As he neared the bench, he could feel Coach's eyes. Max kept his gaze in the other direction. He sat and hung his head for the final sixty seconds.

The Thunder lost, 2-1. As players circled around Coach Pepper, Max could feel every eye on him. Coach spoke. "My word today is 'DISCORD.' It means, 'lack of harmony.' We're not playing as a team. We're also tired. Take Tuesday off, we'll practice only on Thursday. We'll be ready for the Cobras next Saturday."

Max picked up his bag. A big hand landed on his shoulder. "Stay here." Max felt an ache in his ankle, so he sat. Seconds later, Coach stood in front of him.

"I can't believe what I just saw, Max. I've never seen you commit a foul like that. We were back in the game, and then you took us out of it."

"Sorry," Max murmured, but Coach wasn't done. He leveled his eyes on Max. "I told you to keep your cool, and then you go out and commit a reckless foul. That's not what I expect from my captain, Max."

Max kept his eyes on his boots. Finally, he stood and started to walk off, but Coach cuffed his arm. "I heard you run your mouth too."

Max twisted his cleats in the dirt. "I don't get the ball, I don't score. We're losing, and it's my fault."

Coach rested a hand on Max's shoulder. "It's not your fault, Max. Look, you're getting smothered, like bees on honey, remember? It's time for your teammates to step up. They need to accept that you're going to be marked out of games. It's time they learn to play around you."

Coach turned away. Max stomped toward the parking lot, Coach's words echoing in his head. *Play around me? That's just crazy. I make this team go!*

Mr. Miles stepped toward Max, but Max didn't see him, not with his eyes on his laces. When everyone reached the car, Max exploded. "I never get the ball. I yell at everybody. I hate being captain. And now Coach says the team has to do things without me. I wish the season was over."

Mr. Miles tried to find something positive, but this time he came up empty. It was a quiet ride home.

That night, Max paced in his room. *Can't believe I yelled at Fivehead. It's like I turned into Artie.* He tapped a text to his friend. *Meet on the Square?* Fivehead tapped back. *Be over in five.*

A bit later, the boys dropped in the grass. Max took a deep breath. "Sorry I yelled at you, Fiver, really stupid."

"It's okay, Max, I deserved it. You set me up for an easy goal, and I passed to the man on the moon."

Max chuckled. "At least you came close. Me, I didn't sniff the goal."

"Yeah, but you're like the cream in an Oreo, Max, two guys always squeezing ya. The rest of us, we need to play better."

Max plucked a few blades of grass. "Coach says guys have to make things happen without me."

"Well, you can't play next week," Fivehead said. "Maybe guys will do more."

The air went quiet, until Fivehead said, "At least we get to go to New York in a few weeks. You pick your two favorite places yet?"

"Not yet, you?"

"Going to a Yankee game would be cool. So would that boat ride around Manhattan. Maybe we could throw Artie overboard."

Max cackled at that. A few minutes later, he watched Fivehead step to the gate. *I love Fivehead. Even when I feel bad, he cracks me up.*

After dinner, Max went to his room and dug out the list from Coach. He ran his eyes over the six options for New York.

Empire State Building
Statue of Liberty

Yankee Stadium, baseball game
Boat ride around Manhattan
Bronx Zoo
Museum of Natural History

Max went on the Internet and checked out each possibility. He circled his two favorites and tucked the sheet into his soccer bag. Later that night, he checked the league website. The Thunder had one win, one loss, and one tie. They were tied for fifth place. Max had dropped to tenth in the scoring race. He started to check the academy website, but then he logged off. *I already feel like dog-doo. Why should I read about how great Red's doing?*

Max stood and thumped the tennis ball into his wall. *Red's tearin' it up with the Falcons. I'm getting red cards with the Thunder. He doesn't bug me anymore with those emails.* Max rolled over, buried his face in his pillow. *Guess Mom and Betsy were right. I should've joined the Falcons.*

CHAPTER 6

MAXING OUT

THAT NIGHT MAX WOKE IN a cold sweat, his dream still fresh. In it, he was crawling across the desert, in his soccer uniform. A powerful wind roared in Max's face, but it wasn't blowing sand. It was blowing red cards, millions of them. Max sat up. *I got a red card, unreal. I've never even had a yellow card! Now I have to wait two weeks before I play my next game.* Max fell back onto his pillow. *There's only one thing I can do. Whip myself into better shape.*

Max drifted back off. When he woke four hours later, he sat up and tapped his shin. It was sore, but not sore enough to stop him. Looking out on the Square, he saw the grass lit by the first rays of sun. Max put on his soccer gear, sank to his thick carpet, and ran through his stretches. Then he shot downstairs, where he poured a bowl of raisin bran and a glass of milk. He ate fast.

Max stepped onto the deck and opened the ball bin. He took out a ball and a stack of ten yellow cones. He set the cones in a wavy line across the Square. With the ball at his boot, Max decided on his challenge. *I'll go across using only my right boot, and come back using only my left boot.* He took off and blew through all ten cones. But the journey back wasn't so smooth. Using his left foot, Max lost control twice, the ball rolling past the wrong side of a cone. Finally, he made it back across the line. *With my left foot, I need to balance speed with control.* Six more times, Max dribbled back and forth through the cones. With only his left foot, both ways.

After a short rest, Max jogged behind the shed and grabbed a thin board. It was twenty-four feet wide by eight feet high, the size of a goal. Mr. Miles had cut holes in each corner, four targets, three feet by three feet. Max tried to pull the board to the goal, but it kept tipping over. Finally, he grabbed one end, dragged it through the grass, and leaned it against the frame.

Max arranged ten balls in a row, along the chalk eighteen yards from goal. *This is pretty cool, I'm on the Square, shooting at four squares.* First, he took aim at the gap in the upper right corner. Six shots rattled the board, three sailed over the bar, and one flew in the hole. *Not good enough.* Max stuck two in the upper left corner, three in the lower left, and five in the lower right. He did the math. *Eleven out of forty. Twelve, that's my target next time I do this.*

His ball work done, Max set his toes on the chalk. He crouched, clicked his watch, and bolted off. As he dashed across the far line, his watch read 5:13. *I won't quit until I break five seconds.* After five sprints, Max's best time was 5:04. He took his stance, clicked his watch, and took off. Crossing the line, he looked at his wrist. When he saw 4.99, he pumped a fist.

Max picked up his ball and started for the house. Suddenly, he felt a bit woozy. He sank into the grass and gazed up at a few white clouds. A minute later, a voice woke him.

"I've been watching you, Max," Betsy said. "You're scaring me."

"Just tryin' to get better," Max blurted between quick breaths.

"I get it, but you're not some robot. You keep it up, you'll wear yourself to a nub."

"A nub?"

"Yeah, something small and lifeless, like the eraser on a pencil," Betsy said.

"There you go again, with those big words," Max whined.

Betsy snorted. "Nub has only three letters, Max."

"You know what I mean," Max replied.

"You mean, 'uncommon' words?" Betsy asked.

Max rolled his eyes. "There you go again."

On Wednesday, and then again on Friday, Max ran through his workout on the Square. After finishing his workout on Friday, he went inside to find his mom making a stew of baked beans and cut-up hot dogs. Thirty minutes later, Max loaded up his bowl and joined his family on the couch. Mr. Miles flicked on the TV and found a professional soccer match. When it ended, Max sprang off the couch and broke into a dance. "After watching that, I want to play so bad tomorrow." Then he stopped dancing. "But no, I get to collect splinters on the bench."

When Max woke on Saturday morning, he got dressed and grabbed a pen and notepad off his desk. An hour later he sat on the bench at Orchard Park, pen and pad in hand, ready to take on Coach's assignment. The Thunder faced the Cobras, the only undefeated team in the league. In the fourth minute, Fivehead broke free in the box. He beat one guy and cocked his leg to shoot, but another Cobra sliced him to the turf. The ref called a foul and pointed at the spot. Penalty kick for the Thunder.

"Wesley, your kick!" Coach yelled. Max watched as Fivehead set the ball down and backed away. The ref blew his whistle. But Fivehead just stood there, the seconds ticking by. Max felt his pulse jump. *He's so nervous, he never expected to take this.* Finally, Fivehead stepped into a low bolt that clipped the post and flew wide.

Max hung his head. *That's on me.*

Fivehead's errant shot took the rumble out of the Thunder. Five minutes later, the Cobra center back rose high and headed a corner under Theo's hands. Then their striker, the shortest kid on the pitch, dribbled around four foes and cracked a bullet into the corner from twenty yards. When the halftime whistle blew, the Thunder trailed, 2-0. The boys gathered in front of a pacing Coach Pepper. "Boys, you're trying to dribble into the goal. Think about it, how many times do we score from twenty yards in practice? You get an open look from around the box, fire away!"

Coach looked at Max. "Max, you took notes, tell us what you saw."

"We're getting shouldered off the fifty-fifty balls," Max started. "Go in harder, guys."

"Good point," Coach said. "Anything else?"

"We're going up the middle too much," Max went on. "It's bunched up in there. Play the ball out wide, there's lots more space."

Coach nodded. "That it?"

Max checked his notes. "Fiver's put some good balls across the box, but we're not there. We gotta flood the box."

Artie swung his foot through the grass. "Thanks, Max, guess we're a bunch of dorks."

"Hang on, I'm gettin' to the good stuff now," Max replied. "Artie, you're cutting off every ball in the box. And Theo, you're really quick off your line. I mean, you own every cross."

Coach nodded. "Thanks, Max." Coach shared a few more pointers. Then he put out a hand and the boys stacked theirs on top. "Give it all you got, boys, and we'll get back in it."

But the Thunder made little noise in the second half. They lost, 4-0. As Max watched his teammates trudge off the field, he heard his belly groan. *That loss was my fault. No more red cards.*

That Wednesday, Max got home from school and got out his notes for his book report. It was due the next day. He wrote the first paragraph, but then he noticed that his room was getting darker. Stepping to his window, he saw black clouds rolling in. *It's gonna pour, I better run now.*

Max threw on his gear, dropped to his carpet, and stretched. He went down and stepped out the front door, a cool breeze nipping his cheeks. *Time to grind out three miles*. Max set his watch and took off. Half way through his run, the breeze picked up. Over the last mile it blew in his face, but that only made him run harder. As he reached his mailbox, Max checked his watch. 24:05. He shook a fist. *About eight minutes a mile, not bad for running into that wall of wind.*

Walking up his driveway, Max felt the first drops. By the time he reached the garage, it felt like marbles were falling. He grabbed a tall bottle of water off the shelf and guzzled half in one tilt.

A bit later, the Miles family sat down to meat loaf and mashed potatoes. Max's eyelids felt heavy, so did his fork. There was chatter at the table, but Max was in his own zone.

"Max, you're quiet as a scarecrow," Mrs. Miles said.

"I'm thinking about my book report, gotta finish it tonight."

"I saw running clothes by the laundry basket upstairs," Mr. Miles said. "Did you run today?"

"Just three miles."

"No wonder you look half asleep," Mr. Miles shot back. "Why are you running on the day between practices?"

"Come on, Dad, I gotta do more. We have one win, one tie, and two losses."

"Who do you play on Saturday?" Betsy asked.

"The Coyotes," Max answered. "Big game, we need a win before our tournament in New York."

"I just read about that tournament in the paper," Betsy said. "The Falcons are playing in it. They're undefeated. Red Peters has twelve goals, leads the academy league."

"Yeah, and I hope we get to play 'em," Max said. "Might be the one game where I don't get double-teamed."

For dessert, Max split an Oreo, ate half, and put the other half back in the package. Trudging up the stairs, he sat at his desk and pulled out his notes. He finished three sentences, but then his eyes took over. *We're closing now, Max, sorry.*

Max stood and dropped on his bed. *Just a little nap, get some energy back.*

The next time Max opened his eyes, he saw a sliver of sunlight on his blanket. He sat up and checked his clock: 6:03 a.m. *My paper!*

Max vaulted out of bed, sat, and grabbed his pen. Never had he written so fast. A few sentences strayed above the lines, some drifted below. When his hand cramped up, he got up and changed into jeans and a yellow polo shirt. Checking his clock, he shook his head. *Got no time for breakfast.* He scribbled on, until he heard Betsy call out, "I'm leaving for the bus, Max."

Max stuffed his notebook in his backpack and bounded down the stairs. At the door, his mom stuck a banana in his backpack.

"Working on your paper, huh?" Mrs. Miles asked.

"Yeah, my nap turned into a full night's sleep. See ya."

Max hustled out. When he reached the bus stop, he told Fivehead that he had to sit alone.

Fivehead shot him a look. "What, you forget to shower?"

Max snorted. "Gotta finish a paper."

On the ride to school, Max managed to grind out the third page. Later that morning, he walked up and handed it to Miss Rickles. On the way back to his seat, Max could feel his heart hammer on his shirt. *I hope she can read that, I barely can.*

That Friday, Max got his paper back. The grade was written in big red ink, D+. A note was written under it. *See me after class.* Max bowed his head. *First D ever, D as in, 'dog bite.'* When the bell rang, Max waited for the other students to leave. His pulse ticking fast, he walked up to Miss Rickles. She stared into his eyes. "Max, I could barely read your paper. What I could read wasn't worth reading. Is something troubling you?"

Max thought fast. "Uh, I got this bug, Miss Rickles."

"Is that bug called soccer?"

Max's face went blank, and Miss Rickles went on. "Should I talk with your parents?"

"Oh no, I'll do better, promise."

"Darn right you will," she snapped.

Max stood and scooted out. *That's your last D ever, you dope.*

The next morning, Max pulled back his shade and gazed up at blue sky. *I haven't played in two weeks, feels like two years. The Coyotes are gonna pay, I'll make 'em howl in pain.* But an hour later at the field, it was Max feeling the pain. Coach Pepper announced the lineup, and Max wasn't in it. Fivehead stuck up his hand. "Coach, you forgot about Max."

"I've got a surprise for the Coyotes," Coach

explained. "I'll put Max in after three minutes. I'm hoping he can bash one in before the Coyotes know what hit 'em."

As the game started, Max looked at his arm band, marked with the letters, C-A-P-T-A-I-N. He twisted his cleats deep in the dirt. *Why am I on the bench? Coach has lost it.*

When the Coyotes scored in the second minute, Max could feel his pulse bouncing like a jackhammer. Coach waved him over. "Go in, take Sam out." Max sprinted onto the field. A minute later, he gathered a stray ball in the circle. A Coyote ran at him. Max let him get close, and then he dinked the ball through the boy's boots. His eyes up, Max saw a clear path toward the box, and he hit top speed in three strides. As he neared the arc, the center back jockeyed him. Max scissored over the ball. The back lost his balance, and Max surged past.

Reaching the eighteen, Max felt another back closing from the side. He stole a glance at goal. *I see a window, and I'm gonna smash it.* Max lashed a low bullet toward the far corner. The keeper dove, but the ball sizzled past him and stabbed the cords. Max tried to run, but Fivehead tackled him. "Wicked shot, Max!" he yelped.

The Coyotes' coach waved over two midfielders. "That number seven is trouble," he said. "He doesn't touch the ball, got it boys?" The boys nodded.

A minute later, Max ran down a free ball near the circle. He turned, but right into a human fence. Out of the corner of his eye, Max picked up Ben barreling down the left side. He spooned the ball into Ben's path and broke for the box, three Coyotes keeping pace. Ben crossed, but Max was caged in. The keeper caught the ball, and Max tossed up his arms.

His frustration rising, Max ran like a deer to get open. But each time he turned around, he had at least two opponents over his shoulder. In the stands, Betsy turned to her mom. "Max is working so hard."

"But his teammates can't get him the ball," Mrs. Miles griped. "And they can't do anything without him."

As the half wore on, Max tried a different strategy. *If my teammates can't find me, I gotta find the ball.* When a Coyote midfielder dribbled at Max, Max read his eyes. He anticipated a pass, and when it came, he lunged and got his boot on it. Max built speed, tapped his way around three defenders, and cracked a rocket from twenty yards. *Thunk!* The ball stung the far post with such force that it caromed all the way outside the box. A Coyote gathered and accelerated into open space.

Max was bent over, flat out of gas. He watched as one Coyote pushed the ball through the circle and a Coyote wing ran to his right. Artie was the only Thunder player back to defend. When Artie broke for the ball, the Coyote pushed it into his wing's path. As the wing collected near the eighteen, Theo came racing out. The boy looked up and floated the ball over Theo into the far corner. Coyotes 1, Thunder 1.

At halftime, Max dragged his feet to the bench. He grabbed his water bottle and sucked it dry. As Max sat, Coach neared. "Max, you look exhausted. Sit for a bit."

"I just caught my breath, Coach. I'm ready to play."

Coach paused. "Okay, but I got my eye on you."

A minute later, the Thunder caught another piece of hard luck. A Coyote corner kick nicked Artie's arm, and the ref pointed to the penalty spot. The Coyote smashed the ball past Theo, and the Thunder trailed, 2-1. As the clock ticked down, Max ran hard to get free. He got the ball a few times, but was always surrounded. He passed well, but his teammates failed to create any threats. When the Thunder got a throw-in deep in its own half, Max saw his dad wave and put up a single finger. Max drew a deep breath. *Time to do something special.*

As Ben picked up the ball, Max ran back toward his own corner flag. "Ben!" he snapped. Farther up the field everyone was covered, so Ben threw back toward Max. As the ball rolled toward Max, he saw two Coyotes coming at him. *Bring it on.*

Max gathered the ball and built speed. He cut left around the first foe, and then right around the second one. Suddenly, Max veered into open space across the field.

"Get on him!" yelled the Coyotes' coach. But now Max was dribbling at full speed. He reached the far flank and cut up toward the flag. A Coyote midfielder challenged, but Max surged past him. Thirty yards out, Max made a diagonal cut inside. Two Coyotes closed in. Max put three quick touches on the ball, leaving both foes in the dust. He thrust back into high gear and neared the opposing box. The center back slid over, but Max beat him to the outside. He was now fifteen yards from goal, the keeper charging at him. Max faked a shot, dropping the keeper to his knees. He cut wide of the keeper, the open goal yawning at him five yards away. Max had covered over a hundred yards, and left seven Coyotes in his trail. He pulled his leg back to guide the ball home. But then Max fell over, his body thudding to the ground. The ref blew his whistle and ran over. Max lay in the grass, still as a stone.

CHAPTER 7
EXHAUSTED

An hour later, Max blinked out of a nap. Blue walls surrounded him. *My walls are white.* He tilted his head to the window. *That's not my backyard.*

"Max, I'm here."

Max swung his head the other way. His mom leaned forward in her chair and patted his arm.

"Mom, where are we?" Max asked.

"Chelsea Hospital, Max."

"What happened?"

"You passed out on the field."

Max pushed up his eyebrows. "No way."

"Do you remember the end of your game?" she asked.

"What game?"

"You played a game today, Max. You were

behind by one goal. In the last minute, you took a throw-in deep in your own end. You beat a few guys, then you cut across to the other side. You beat a few more guys, broke free into the box. The keeper came out. You dribbled around him. You cocked your leg to shoot, and that's when you crumpled to the ground."

"Wow, I don't remember any of that. You mean, I just fell over on my own?"

"Yep, and you didn't get up. We were scared, Max. What a relief to see you're okay."

"So why did I pass out?"

"You have a case of exhaustion."

Max crinkled his nose. "What's that mean?"

"You pushed yourself until your body gave out, Max."

Max blinked a few times. "Did we score at the end?"

"No, the keeper ran back and dove on the ball. You guys lost, two to one."

"So, I passed out for no good reason?"

Mrs. Miles smiled. "At least you haven't exhausted your wit."

"Where's Dad and Betsy?" Max asked.

"Dad took Betsy to her game. They should be here soon."

Max noticed a thin tube attached to his arm. "That tube gives me the creeps."

"They're pumping in nutrients," Mrs. Miles said.

A man wearing a white coat stepped in. Max noticed his name tag, 'Doctor Ellis.'

"How are you feeling, Max?" the doctor asked.

"Embarrassed," Max said.

The doctor cocked his head sideways. "Why's that?"

"I passed out during a game, pretty wimpy."

"Nothing wimpy about it, Max," Dr. Ellis replied. "I'd say you left it all on the field."

"Maybe, but I can't believe this. I thought I was fit."

"You're fit as a fiddle, Max," the doctor countered. "The thing is, we all have limits. Your mom says you've been pushing yourself hard, every day. Even professional soccer players don't do that."

"They don't?"

"The pros play a match on Saturday," Dr. Ellis said. "They rest on Sunday. They take it easy at practice on Monday. Think about that.

One hard day, two easy days. If the pros don't push themselves every day, why should you?"

Max blew out a sigh. "I always have two guys on me, sometimes three. I figured I have to run the whole game."

"I like your spirit, Max," the doctor said. "But you can't help your team from a hospital bed."

Dr. Ellis looked at Mrs. Miles, and then back at Max. "We need to talk about something else, Max. Your eating habits. Your mom says you haven't been finishing your dinner. Are you snacking between meals?"

Max thought for a bit. *Better tell the truth.* "Sometimes I get hungry before lunch at school. The vending machine catches my eye. It's like a magnet, pulling me over. I slip in a few quarters and my finger goes straight to the button for Reese's Cups."

"Max, I had no idea," his mom said.

"Snickers is a close second," Max added.

Dr. Ellis fought off a grin. "Okay, how about later in the day?" he asked.

"One of my nicknames is, 'Chip,'" Max said. "After school, I usually crush a bag of corn chips, sometimes two."

Max saw his mom's eyes bulge. He put up his hands. "Corn's good for ya, right?"

"There's not much corn in those chips, Max," Dr. Ellis replied. "And what do you drink with those chips?"

"Grape soda, but only one can."

Mrs. Miles shook her head. "No wonder you don't finish your dinner."

Dr. Ellis kept going. "What about on weekends?"

"Same stuff, just more volume," Max replied. "But doctor, I work that stuff off, right?"

"It's not that simple, Max," Dr. Ellis answered. "Some foods are good for you, some are not good. Think about the gas you put in a car. If you put in the best fuel, your car runs smoothly. If you put in cheap fuel, your car makes funny noises. From now on, you will eat the right foods, and always be fueled up."

"We'll talk more about that at home, Max," Mrs. Miles said.

Can't wait, Max thought.

A bit later, the doctor studied Max's eyes with a small flashlight. Then he checked his pulse, and he gave Max a thumbs-up. "You're good to go home tonight, Max."

Max pumped a fist, but then Dr. Ellis stole Max's joy. "I want you to lay low for a week," he told Max. "No exercise, except for walking."

Max made a face. "But what about my soccer?"

"Not for a week, Max," Dr. Ellis said. He left the room, and Max looked at his mom.

"You know I heal quick, Mom. I'll be good in a couple days."

"Doctor Ellis knows best, Max."

Max gnashed his teeth. A bit later, he was nibbling on a salted cracker when his dad and Betsy walked in. "How are you feeling, Max?" Mr. Miles asked.

"Much better, Dad. But get this, the doctor wants me to take a week off. Thing is, I know I'll be ready for practice on Tuesday."

Mr. Miles gave Max his 'cut the baloney' stare.

Max noticed a splotch of dirt on Betsy's shirt. "How'd you do?" he asked.

Betsy put up a thumb. "We fell behind by three goals but came back to win, five-four."

"Sounds like a wild game," Max said. "You must be exhausted."

Betsy smiled. "Good one, Max."

A half-hour later, Max got released. His family at his side, he stepped through the revolving door and walked slowly toward the car. As he reached the lot, Max looked over his shoulder. *Place is kinda creepy. Quiet, so many sad faces, weird smell in the air. But they took care of me, right?*

Back at his house, Max found a note taped to the front door. *Dude, you made the greatest run I've ever seen. You dribbled around like, ten Coyotes. No wonder you ran outta gas! - Fiver*

Max smiled. Then his dad tapped him on the shoulder. "Time for a talk."

Max cringed. *I hate those words*. He followed his parents into the family room, and they sat on the couch. Mrs. Miles draped an arm on Max's shoulder. "When I saw you go down, a chill ran up my spine."

"Talk about bad timing," Max said. "A few more seconds, and I woulda tied the game."

"We're going to make sure that never happens again," Mr. Miles said. "First, you will not work out hard two days in a row. That means that after every practice and every game, you will take it easy the next day."

"But I'll go backward."

"No, you won't," Mr. Miles volleyed. "Look, you already run more than any other player, by a mile."

Max couldn't argue with that.

"Your diet is going to change, too," Mrs. Miles went on. "No more chips, no more soda. You're going to start loading up on healthy carbohydrates."

"Never had one," Max said.

"A carbohydrate isn't a kind of food, Max, but it is found in food," Mrs. Miles explained. "It's a compound made up of carbon, hydrogen, and oxygen."

Max put up his hands. "Mom, you gotta chill out. First, 'carbohydrate,' then 'compound.' Big words, too big for me."

"Here's my point, Max. You'll be eating lots of bread, pasta, rice, and cereal."

"I'm good with that," Max said.

Mrs. Miles wasn't done. "From now on, you will eat a meal at least two hours before your games. That will give you energy, and the time you need to digest your meal."

Max nodded and started to get up, but his dad pointed him back to the couch.

"Your body is seventy percent water, Max," his dad said. "During a game, you sweat off a lot of water. You need to hydrate – keep your water levels up. You will drink two bottles with your pre-game meal. At halftime, you drink another half-bottle. After the game, another full bottle."

"You'll need a wheelbarrow to get me to the car."

"One more thing, Max," Mrs. Miles added. "You love fruit, and fruit's good for you, so we'll start making fruit smoothies."

"Smoothies?"

"They're like milk shakes, only with fruit," she explained. "We can use bananas, strawberries, oranges, tangerines, blueberries, the list goes on."

"Maybe I can get Fivehead to help," Max said. "So, is class over now?"

"As long as you understand your assignments," his dad said.

Max got up and stepped into the kitchen. Betsy handed him the paper. "More headlines about your best friend," she said.

Max glanced at the page.

PETERS SCORES FOURTH HAT TRICK FOR FALCONS

Max didn't bother to read the story. He plodded up the stairs and sank onto his bed. *We never win, and the Falcons never lose. I used to think I wanted to play against them in New York. Maybe that's not such a good idea.*

CHAPTER 8

'SMOOTH' MOVE

FOR THE NEXT FIVE DAYS, Max only walked. Not a single long stride. He took the stairs one at a time, not his usual two. Not once did he touch a soccer ball, or a tennis ball. He felt like he was moving in slow motion. But with each day he felt a little stronger – and a lot more antsy.

Walking home from the bus on Friday, Max saw his mom unloading groceries from the car. He grabbed the last bag, walked in, and set it on the kitchen counter.

"Thanks, Max," Mrs. Miles said. "How are you feeling?"

"Feelin' great, Mom. Sun's out, perfect day for a short run."

Mrs. Miles saw that coming. "Not yet, Max.

Doctor Ellis said seven days. Two more to go, and then on Monday, you're free."

Max frowned. "Come on, Mom, I've been running all week. Running out of patience."

His mom chuckled. "Here's an idea, Max. Do your homework, then I'll take you and Wesley to the store. You can pick up the ingredients for banana smoothies, and I'll help you make them for dinner."

"I don't have much homework."

"What about that paper for your trip to New York?"

"I started it already."

"So, finish it. We'll go in an hour."

Max grabbed his backpack and dragged his feet up to his room. He flipped open his notebook and reviewed his notes. *I got more work to do.* He turned on his computer, studied a few more websites, and jotted more notes. Finally, he began to write. *A paleontologist studies fossils. Fossils are the remains of extinct animals. A fossil can contain teeth, bone or shell, or even a footprint. Most fossils are found in rocks.*

Max kept writing. An hour passed quickly. He closed his book, grabbed his phone, and tapped a text to Fivehead. *Wanna make banana smoothies for dinner tonight?*

Fivehead: *I'm allergic to cooking.*

Max: *It's not cooking, we just throw some stuff in the blender.*

Fivehead: *My parents got the kitchen covered. Three's a crowd, right?*

Max: *Come on, my mom will take us to the store to get the stuff.*

Fivehead: *If I learn how to cook, my parents will expect me to make all the meals.*

With that, Max gave up. He went down to the kitchen, where his mom was scribbling out a list.

"Is Wesley joining us?" she asked.

"He blew me off."

Mrs. Miles finished the list and handed it to Max. "Let's hit the supermarket."

Max followed his mom outside. Suddenly, a voice boomed out from up the sidewalk. "Smoothie man's comin', Smoothie man's comin'!"

Max saw Fivehead jogging at him, a big white chef's hat bouncing on his head. As Fivehead reached Max, he bent over to catch his breath. His hat fell off. He scooped it up with his sneaker, and then he and Max gave each other five.

"I thought you weren't coming," Max said.

"My mom told me to rake the backyard," Fivehead answered. "I told her we were going shopping, that we're makin' smoothies. She was so pumped, she said she'd rake the yard."

Max snorted. Mrs. Miles looked at Fivehead. "So, Wesley, where'd you get that cool hat?"

"My mom wore it to some Halloween party," Fivehead said. "She can be a little goofy."

A bit later, Mrs. Miles and the boys rolled up to the store. Mrs. Miles gave Max some money. She stayed in the car, and so did Fivehead's hat. Max got out and grabbed a cart, and Fivehead followed him inside. The list in his hand, Max led Fivehead to the banana stand. Fivehead grabbed a bunch and set them in the cart. Max studied the bananas, and then he lifted the bunch out and put it back.

"Those are too green, Fiver."

Fivehead puffed out a cheek full of air. "You're bananas, Max."

Fivehead found a more yellow bunch and set it in the cart. Max eyed that bunch and shook his head. "My mom says the best bananas have brown flecks on 'em."

Fivehead made a face. "Flecks?"

"You know, spots," Max explained.

"Okay, just speak English."

Fivehead put back the second bunch. He pulled out another cluster of four, each one speckled with brown dots. "Perfect," Max said.

Max checked his list. "Yogurt." Fivehead darted off, and Max caught up in the dairy aisle. Fivehead swung his hands at the shelves. "There's like, three hundred kinds."

"Two cups of low-fat vanilla," Max said.

Fivehead grabbed two cups and set them in the cart. Max eyed the labels, and handed both cups back to Fivehead.

"I said, 'low fat.'"

Fivehead tossed his head back. "See why I never go shopping?" He found the low-fat section and put two containers in the cart. Max checked his list.

"One more thing, a bag of crushed ice."

Fivehead squinted at Max. "We makin' a Smoothie, or an igloo?"

Max laughed. "Just goin' by the list, Fiver."

Fivehead found the freezer, pulled out a bag of ice, and put it in the cart.

"All set," Max said.

"Not yet," Fivehead snapped. "Two more things, follow me."

Max watched Fivehead peel away. *What is that knucklehead up to now?* Max wheeled the cart after his friend. He found him two aisles over, in the peanut butter section. Fivehead grabbed a jar and put it in the cart.

"Peanut butter's not on the list," Max said.

"Come on, Max, everything's better with peanut butter. I mean, you ever spread peanut butter on a banana? You can barely taste the banana."

Fivehead tore off to another aisle. Max finally found him, holding a bag of double-stuffed cookies.

"No way," Max said.

"Come on, Max, these go with everything, you know it."

"Put it back, we don't have enough money."

Fivehead kissed the bag and put it back. The boys paid for their groceries and hustled back to the car.

"Get everything?" Mrs. Miles asked.

"Yup," Max said. Fivehead added, "Plus, we got a special ingredient."

"I'm afraid to guess," Mrs. Miles answered.

"Peanut butter," Max said.

Mrs. Miles thought for a second. "That should work."

Fivehead flicked the back of Max's ear. "Told ya."

Back at the house Max got out the blender, and he and Fivehead spooned in the yogurt. Mrs. Miles cut the bananas into small pieces and tossed them in.

"How much peanut butter do we put in?" Max asked.

"The whole jar," Fivehead cracked.

"Not quite," Mrs. Miles said. She eyed the jar, saw it held twelve ounces. "Scoop one fourth of the way down." The boys took turns spooning peanut butter into the blender. Next, Mrs. Miles measured out two cups of crushed ice and dumped them in. She put on the lid. "Okay, Max, mix," she said.

Max hit the button, and he and Fivehead watched their dinner spin to life. After fifteen seconds, Max shut it off. He filled two tall glasses. Fivehead took the first sip. "Wow, this is creamy, kinda like a milk shake."

"Go slow, boys," Mrs. Miles warned. "You drink it too fast, you'll get a headache."

Max took a long slurp. "Mom, this is crazy good."

"That's a quick and healthy meal, boys," she said. "Takes just four ingredients and ten minutes. It has plenty of protein, calcium and other nutrients - instant energy."

Max took another gulp. "Bet we can make all kinds of smoothies." His mom reached into the cupboard and took out a bag of sunflower seeds. Shaking it, she said, "Next time, we'll use sunflower seeds instead of peanut butter."

Fivehead shook his head. "You mean sunflower seeds *and* peanut butter."

Later that night, Max talked his parents into letting him tap a ball with Fivehead on the Square. After a few minutes, Fivehead scooped up the ball. "Max, you're ready to play tomorrow, I know it, you know it. It's time you ask your parents, right?"

Max made a sour face. "Not gonna work, Fiver."

"It's worth a try, Max."

Max shrugged. "Guess so, but my only chance is my mom. You gotta come with me."

Fivehead followed Max inside, where his parents sat at the kitchen table. Max and Fivehead sat with them. Max took a deep breath, but Mr. Miles spoke first.

"No," he said.

Max snorted, and then he eyed his mom. "How about just half the game?" he asked.

"We're sticking with the doctor's orders," his mom said. "You're on the sideline until Monday."

"Max looks ready to me," Fivehead blurted.

Mr. Miles looked over his glasses at Fivehead. Fivehead put up his hands. "Just sayin'."

Laughter rang out. Then Mr. Miles spoke. "This conversation is over."

Max felt an urge to argue, but why waste words?

The next day, Max arrived at Orchard Park with a knot in his stomach. *Before this season, I hardly*

missed a game in my life. Now, I'm about to miss my second one in three weeks. After the pre-game huddle, Max sat at the end of the bench and scraped his heels on the grass.

From the first whistle, the Thunder got outplayed in the middle. They fell behind three-nil until Fivehead fired in a long screamer in the dying minutes. Ben hit the bar seconds later, but that was the Thunder's last crack. Final score: Bobcats 3, Thunder 1.

Afterward, Coach Pepper paced in front of the team. "My word is 'TENACIOUS,'" Coach said. "It means sticking to your task and never giving up. Today we got down three, but we got one back and made them sweat. I'm proud of the way you hung in there."

But Artie wasn't buying it. "Coach, we're a mess. We can't keep the ball, we can't pass, and we hardly sniff the other goal."

Max felt his chest hammer. "You can't get down, Artie."

"We can't get up, Max," Artie snapped back.

"That's enough, Artie," Coach cut in. "Look, next week, we play the Fury. They're only one game ahead of us. What are we gonna do?"

"We're gonna win!" Max blared.

No one else said anything. Max scanned the eyes around him. *Wow, the guys really look defeated.*

When Max's alarm rang on Monday, he bounced out of bed and pumped a fist. *I'm free at last!* He celebrated by jogging to the bus stop. As the week unfolded, Max stepped into his new routine. He legged out a short, easy jog on Monday, went to practice on Tuesday and Thursday, and laid low on Wednesday and Friday.

At last, Saturday came. Max woke to sunlight on his comforter. He slid out, dropped to his carpet, and ran through his stretches. Throwing on his uniform in record time, he checked himself in the mirror. *Keep your mouth shut today, Max.*

Two hours later, Mr. Miles drove into the lot by the field. "Remember, Max, stay calm," Betsy said.

"And catch your breath after long runs," Mr. Miles added.

"Drink lots of water at halftime," piled on his mom.

When Mr. Miles eased the car into a parking space, Max sprang out. He was the first player to reach the bench. He dropped his bag and set off for a warm-up jog. Max could tell the bright white chalk had just been put down that morning. *Man, I love being out here. I can't miss another game, ever.*

A bit later, the boys gathered around Coach Pepper. "Our first option is Max in the middle," he said. "If he's bottled up, find the open player and run off your pass." Coach put out his big hand and the boys piled theirs on top. "Three, two, one, Thunder!"

In the opening minute, Artie rose high and nodded out a corner kick. Max beat a foe to it and shot up the flank. As a defender neared, he fed Ben in the circle. Ben one-timed down the line, Fivehead in hot pursuit. As Fivehead gathered the ball, Max bolted up the middle. Fivehead cut inside his man and barreled toward the box. Max was now running even with him, heading for the arc. Fivehead rolled the ball ahead of Max. Max ran on and lashed a low dart. The keeper dove, but the ball whistled past his fingers and stabbed the far corner. Max felt that thump-thump-thump in his chest, but only for a second.

The whistle blew. The ref called Max offside, and he waved off the goal. Max ran to the ref. "But I was even with the back when the ball was played!" Max pleaded.

"My linesman saw it, he made the call," the ref said.

"Your linesman's blind!" Max wailed.

Another whistle. The ref stepped to Max and showed him a yellow card.

Now Max had lost control. "Ref, that's –"

"Max!" yelled Fivehead.

His chin on his chest, Max jogged back to the circle. *This is crazy, even the refs are against me. Doesn't matter, no one's gonna stop me.* A minute later, a Fury back sent a towering goal kick Max's way. He leaped over a foe and headed the ball up the right flank. Ben ran it down, and Max sprinted for the box. A hand grabbed Max's shirt, but he swatted it off. As he neared the arc, Ben's cross curled in from the corner. Max cut inside the center back and swung into a volley. It was a clean strike, but the keeper dove and fingered the ball inches wide.

Max threw his head back, but now his

adrenaline was pumping full bore. A bit later, he latched onto a loose ball, carved a path around two foes, and ripped a rocket. The ball stung the bar and hopped over, and this time Max fell to his knees. *I got the worst luck in the world!*

At halftime, the Thunder jogged off in a scoreless tie. As Max drained his water bottle, Ben stepped over. "You're playin' great, Max, wow."

"Thanks, Ben, but we still got a goose egg on the board. Look, you're faster than the guy marking you. I'll lead you into the corner and crash the box." Ben held up his palm and Max smacked it.

Coach Pepper called the team in. "You're moving the ball well, boys," he said. "Keep it up, we'll break through."

Five minutes into the second half, Max made a clean tackle in the circle. Without looking up, he lofted a ball ahead of Ben. As Ben surged after it, Max tore for goal. Ben beat his foe to the ball. With open grass ahead, Ben tapped once into box and cracked a pill. The ball sizzled past the keeper, clanked the far post, and bounced out by the penalty spot. Max was only a few yards away. His heart thumping, he took two steps and drilled a dart smack into the corner. The Thunder had scored its first goal in over one hundred and twenty minutes.

But the Fury fought back. Pushing more players forward, they stormed the Thunder's goal. In the last minute, Artie rose high and headed a cross out of the box. A Fury back ran on and struck a hard shot. Theo leaped and tipped the ball into the bar. It ricocheted right to another Fury player, just ten yards off the line. Max was five yards away, too far. But Theo had his eyes on the ball. As he ran at it, the Fury player unloaded. The shot struck Theo flush on the forehead. The ball landed outside the box, and Theo landed on his rear. Fivehead thumped the ball into the Fury half, and the ref blew his final whistle. Thunder 1, Fury 0.

The Thunder swarmed around Theo. Max and Fivehead lifted him up and carried him off the field. Near the bench, the boys gathered around Coach Pepper. Coach set his eyes on Theo, and the huge red welt on his forehead. "Theo, my word for the day is for you," Coach began. "The word is 'LIONHEARTED.' It means brave and determined, and that's what you were on that last shot."

"Thanks, Coach, but I wasn't brave," Theo said. "I never saw the shot."

Fivehead looked at Theo. "Dude, now I know why your parents named you, 'Theo.' Think about it. Your name starts with 'the', and then comes an 'o', or a zero. So, your name is really, 'the shutout.' Get it?"

A few boys nodded. Coach smiled. "Pretty good, Wesley. So, boys, next Saturday, we face the Stallions. They lead the league, but I think you're ready."

"We can beat 'em," Fivehead blared, "I know it."

"Fiver, Fiver, Fiver," the boys chanted.

Coach opened his backpack and pulled out a large red apple. "Our trip to the Big Apple is coming up. How are you guys doing on your projects?"

Coach let the silence hang for a few beats. "Time is ticking away, boys. Remember, on the bus to New York, you will present your topics. So, get on it!"

"What about you, Coach?" Fivehead cracked. "We haven't heard any of your cool facts yet."

Coach fixed a glare on Fivehead. "I'll start quizzing you next week," Coach said. "You guys should study up. Anyone who answers my questions gets a free ice cream in New York."

"Sweet," Fivehead said. "You want to give us some clues?"

"Do some research, Wesley," Coach replied. "You know, stretch your brain."

Fivehead winced. "That hurts, just thinkin' about it."

The boys howled.

On the ride home, Max munched on a bag of trail mix. Mrs. Miles turned to him. "Maybe you guys will get some ink in the newspaper tomorrow."

"We better," Max said, "or it's time to cancel the Chelsea Chimes."

CHAPTER 9

MAX BLOWS UP

THE NEXT MORNING, A CHILLY wind stung Max's face as he stepped out for the paper. He hustled back in and pulled out the sports section. His eyes settled on a large photo of a red-haired boy, swinging his boot into the ball. Max read the caption. *Red Peters buried three goals as the Falcons put out the Fire, 5-0, yesterday. The Falcons are now 11-0, and Peters leads the academy league with twenty goals and nine assists.*

Max gnashed his teeth. *Does Red ever have a bad game?* Then he flipped through the section, searching for a story on his game. He finally found it, tucked low in the corner of the back page. *Thunder wins, 1-0.* When Max read the first sentence, he thought his eyes were playing tricks on him. He read it again. *Wesley Cannon scored the only goal as the Thunder beat the Fury, 1-0, at Freedom Park yesterday.* Max felt a bolt of anger. *I scored the goal, and I'm not Wesley Cannon. I don't even look like Fivehead. How could they get that wrong?*

Max flipped the paper onto the kitchen table. *Red Peters, that piece of dirt is the leading scorer on an undefeated team. A team I coulda joined! Me, I'm playing for a team in sixth place.*

Mrs. Miles walked in and saw the paper. "How's the story on your game, Max?"

"It's short and it's wrong," Max sniped. "It says Fivehead scored the goal."

"That's crazy," Mrs. Miles replied. She leaned in and scanned the front page. "Wow, Red Peters is flying high with the Falcons."

"He shouldn't even be on the Falcons!" Max squawked.

Mrs. Miles tried to find some soothing words, but came up empty. Instead, she opened the cupboard, pulled out a bag of shelled sunflower seeds, and tossed it to Max. "Let's make a smoothie."

Max gave his mom a hand. They lined up a quarter cup of seeds, two cups of skim milk, two chopped bananas, and a half cup of vanilla yogurt. Mrs. Miles measured out one tablespoon of honey, and a teaspoon of cinnamon. Max loaded up the blender, hit the 'on' button, and watched his smoothie blur into form. After ten seconds, he shut it off and filled a tall glass.

"Stick it in the fridge, give it twenty minutes to cool," his mom said.

Max opened the fridge and stuck in the glass. "This'll be the longest twenty minutes ever, Mom."

"I know how you can spend it, Max. Go up and work on your paper for New York."

"Not due for a while," Max said.

"Do it now, Max, for two reasons," his mom shot back. "One, you'll feel good to get it done. And two, it won't hang over your head."

Max climbed up to his room, got out his notes, and wrote. About every four minutes, he checked his watch. When twenty minutes had passed, he tallied up his progress. *Got two hundred words done, almost there.* Max went down and got out his smoothie. The glass was cold. He joined his Mom at the table, took a sip, and smacked his lips. "This is even better than the first one we made."

Mrs. Miles smiled. "Next time, we'll make an orange creamsicle smoothie."

Max tried to pace himself, but he lost. His glass was soon empty. He went back to his room, got on his computer, and did a search on *New York City, fun facts*. For thirty minutes he poked around and jotted notes. *I feel a free cone comin' my way.*

After practice that Tuesday, Coach Pepper called the boys in. His clipboard in hand, he said, "Okay, time to take a bite of the Big Apple. Anyone know how many languages are spoken in New York?"

"Twenty?" Fivehead guessed.

"Not even close."

"Fifty," Ben tried.

"Still a mile off," Coach said.

Max rubbed his forehead. *I know I read this.* He put up his hand and said, "Eight hundred?"

Coach smiled. "Max, you just earned the first free cone in New York. By the way, in about half of the homes in New York, families speak a language that isn't English."

"That's weird," Fivehead yapped. "What do they speak?"

"Spanish is the second most common language," Coach said. "Then comes Chinese, French, and Russian."

Coach checked his clipboard. "One building in New York City has its own zip code. Anyone know which building?"

Ben beat Max to it. "The Empire State Building," he said.

"Cone for Ben!" Coach yelled. "So, Ben, you know why that building has its own zip code?"

"Because it's so huge?" Ben guessed.

"Sort of," Coach said. "Can anybody help Ben?"

Max spoke. "There are a thousand businesses in that building. It's the second biggest office building in the country. Only the Pentagon is bigger."

"Max, you're on fire!" Coach raved. "You get two scoops on that cone."

Coach went on. "What's the tallest building in New York City?"

Fivehead stuck up a hand. "The Empire State Building?"

"You hit the post, Fiver," Coach said. "It's the third tallest."

Ben was next. "Is it the new World Trade Center building?"

"A second scoop for Ben! That's the tallest building in the United States. It's a hundred and four stories high. That's about six soccer fields stacked on top of each other."

Coach set his clipboard on the bench. "Max and Ben, good work. As for the rest of you, you'll get a few more shots at free ice cream, so study up!"

Max grabbed his bag and started for the lot. *I did my homework, and it paid off. Pretty cool.*

On the drive to the field that Saturday, Betsy turned to Max. "Who do you play today?" she asked.

"The Stallions. They lead the league, could be ugly."

"Come on, Max, be positive," Mr. Miles snapped. "Maybe they won't put two guys on you."

Max said nothing. *Yeah, and some day maybe elephants will fly.*

A bit later, Max played the kickoff ahead of Fivehead out wide. Fivehead tried to take on the left back, but the back stripped the ball clean and punched a long, high ball up the flank. As the Stallions wing gathered near the corner, Max felt a cleat stab the top of his boot.

"Yeow!" Max wailed. While he hopped on one foot, his opponent took off for the box. Max eased back into his stride, but by now the wing had sent a return ball to Max's man near the arc. Max could only watch as the Stallion collected and fired a riser that skimmed the bar and flew over. Max locked eyes with his foe.

"Stay off my cleats, punk," Max snapped. The boy spat near Max's boot and jogged off. Max felt a bolt shoot through him.

Theo's goal kick got knocked around in the circle before Max took control. He turned to find one player rushing at him. Max dinked the ball through his foe's boots and burst ahead. Seeing Ben sprint free on the flank, Max led him toward the corner. As Ben met the ball, Max darted for the near side of the box. "Ben!" he called.

Ben fed Max at the corner of the box. A defender challenged, but Max slithered past him. Now he was in alone, but his angle was tight. As the keeper charged out, Max spotted Fivehead streaking toward the far post. He played a soft roller across the goalmouth into Fivehead's path. Fivehead met the ball ten yards from the open goal, but he thumped when he should've tapped. The ball flew into the bar and bounced over.

Fivehead covered his face. Max ran over and tapped his shoulder. "Forget that one, Fiver."

Two minutes before the half, Max flagged a loose ball and carved a path around three Stallions. When the center back met Max, he laid the ball to Ben at the eighteen. Ben cracked a hard shot, but it flew into the keeper's hands. Max felt a pang of anger. *I keep setting guys up, but no one can hit the net.*

Just before halftime, Max caught a break. A Stallions defender slipped on a patch of mud as he tried to boot out a cross. The ball flew straight to Max, just past the arc. Max cushioned it on his chest. As the ball dropped, he stole a quick glance and saw the keeper way off his line. Max swung his right boot into the bottom of the falling ball. The keeper never moved. The ball looped over him and brushed the net inches below the bar.

Fivehead ran over and jumped on Max. "That was some rainbow, Max!" he yelped. A bit later Max trotted off at halftime, and Coach Pepper stepped out to greet him. "You're controlling the game, Max," Coach said. "For once, you got only one guy on you."

But when the second half started, Max had more company. On his first touch, two players charged at him. His eyes up, Max lofted the ball ahead of Fivehead on the flank. Fivehead gathered the pass, sped into the corner, and thumped a long ball for Ben at the back post. Ben ran on and headed the ball just over the bar.

That's when a loud, angry voice boomed across the field. "Get in the game, Stallions!" their coach hollered. His players responded. They began to win every loose ball. Keeping the ball on the grass, the Stallions passed their way around the Thunder. They tied the game with ten minutes to play, and two minutes later they struck again for the lead.

Max had seen little of the ball, and his patience had worn thin. *Time to attack.* When the ball got played to the left back, Max sprang at him. The back tried to beat Max, but Max made a clean tackle. He tapped to Fivehead and bolted up the flank. "Fiver!" Max called. Fivehead tried to hit Max, but a Stallion stole the pass. Max felt his chest pound. *My teammates keep messing up!*

Minutes later, Max cushioned a goal kick on his chest. When two players ran at him, he put three quick touches on the ball and darted free. As Max bore down on the center back at the top of the box, he spied Fivehead free on the flank. When the back challenged Max, he tapped a soft feed into Fivehead's lane ten yards from goal. Fivehead ran on and smashed the ball into the side netting. *Come on, Fiver!* Max muttered under his breath.

A bit later, Max looked over at his dad. He put up one finger and curled it in half. *I got less than a minute to even the score.*

The Stallions keeper smashed the goal kick high and far. Max backed up, outjumped a Stallion, and headed wide to Ben. As Ben controlled, Max exploded into space down the flank. Ben flicked the ball toward the chalk, and Max was on it in a flash.

Max looked up at a lone defender between him and the goal. To his left, he spotted Fivehead dashing toward the far post. "Max, now!"

Fivehead called. But Max had his mind made up. He slashed wide of the defender and let fly from fifteen yards. *Go in, ball!* Max whispered. It sizzled past the keeper, nicked the far post, and sailed out of bounds. The ref looked at his watch and blew his whistle. Game over.

Fivehead ran up and got in Max's face. "I had an open goal, Max!"

"I had a good shot," Max retorted.

"Yeah, and you missed," Fivehead shot back. "What's wrong with you?"

Max's eyes flared. "I set you up for easy goals all game, Fiver. You didn't score once!"

Fivehead's jaw fell open. He turned and stomped toward the bench. Max closed his eyes. *That was really stupid, Max.* For a few seconds he just stood there, his chest flapping on his shirt. *Maybe I can go straight to the car. Nah, gotta get my bag.* Finally, Max walked over and joined the huddle around Coach Pepper. Before Coach could speak, Fivehead beat him to it. "No way we shoulda lost," he snapped, "but somebody forgot how to pass."

Artie piled on. "Yeah, and we all know who that was."

"That's enough!" Coach yelled, a vein

bulging in his neck. He took off his hat and threw it down. "If I hear anyone else criticize a teammate, that player will sit!" Coach paced until he had chosen his next words. "Look, I'm proud of your effort," he said. "The Stallions lead the league, and you made them sweat until the final whistle." Coach picked up his hat and slipped it on. "We had lots of chances, we just can't find the target. We'll fix that at practice on Tuesday. That's it, boys."

Max stepped toward his bag. *Coach is gonna ball me out, I know it.* But then he saw Coach Pepper, taking long strides toward his car. Max reached the lot a minute later, the car already running. Max got in. "You played great today," Mr. Miles said. "Your teammates let you down."

Max dug his fingers into his forehead. "The guys just yelled at me for not passing at the end."

Betsy turned to Max. "I don't blame you for shooting," she said. "You coulda had a bunch of assists, but your teammates can't shoot straight."

"Betsy's right, Max," Mrs. Miles added. "The truth is, you're too good for this team."

Max unstrapped a shin guard. "I barked at

people the whole game. At the end, I got into it with Fivehead. Man, I hate it when people are mad at me."

"This will blow over, Max," his dad said. "When we get home, you can mend fences with Fivehead."

"You mean he can mend fences with me."

"You're the captain, Max," his dad shot back. "It's on you to reach out."

Max sighed. *I knew I never wanted to be captain.*

After dinner that night, Max sat on his bed, squeezing his phone. *Get it over with, Max.* He punched in Fivehead's number.

"Hey, Max," Fivehead answered.

"Sorry I yelled at you, Fiver."

"I deserved it, Max. I wasted so many chances."

"But I was wrong. If I had passed on the last play, bet you woulda scored."

"It's over, Max, we're cool."

Max clicked off and dropped on his bed. *Fiver made that easy for me. But man, I can't be yelling at my teammates anymore.*

Later that night, Max checked his email and

found a message from Coach Pepper. He read. *Boys, I'm sorry I lost my cool after the game. Like you, I was frustrated. We played a great game, but we didn't get the result we deserved. I know there were some hard feelings about how the game ended. Look, Max had to make a quick decision. He trusted his shot and hit the post, a chance well taken. My word for the day is, 'REBOUND.' It means 'overcome a setback' and that's what we'll do in New York next weekend. It's time to take a bite out of the Big Apple. Go Thunder!*

Max hit the reply button. *Coach, thanks, but I shoulda passed. Plus, I yelled at Fivehead after the game. I called him and apologized. From now on, I'll try to act like a captain should.*

Max swung his eyes to his calendar. Then he dropped back on his bed. *We have our trip to New York, and then the spring season is over. For the first time ever, I actually want my soccer season to end.*

CHAPTER 10

ROAD TRIP

On Tuesday, Coach Pepper ran the Thunder through a series of shooting drills. During the last drill, Max lashed a rocket past a diving Theo into the far corner. Theo got up and yanked off his gloves. "I surrender, Coach. I've faced two hundred and twenty shots, I counted."

Coach blew his whistle, and the boys gathered around. When Coach began to pace, Fivehead swung his foot through the grass. "You're pacing, Coach, that means we're about to get a lecture."

"Yep, a lecture on shooting, so pay attention," Coach replied. "Think about this, boys. A good shot starts with your brain. Before you shoot, glance at the goal, pick your spot, and aim at that target."

"You make it sound easy, Coach," Fivehead replied. "But sometimes you don't have time."

"Fair enough," Coach agreed. "If you don't have time to sneak a peek, shoot low to the far post."

"Why's that?" Fivehead asked.

"I'll give you four reasons," Coach answered. "First, it's hard for a keeper to reach low balls. Second, if the keeper gives up a rebound, it might spill into the goalmouth. Third, your shot may hit someone and deflect in. And fourth, if you shoot wide, a teammate may be able to steer the ball into the goal."

Coach let all that sink in. Then he made one more point. "None of those four things can happen if you shoot for the near post and miss wide."

Max nodded at Coach's words. *Wow, I never thought about that.*

Ben raised a hand. "Coach, does that mean we should never shoot to the near post?"

"I'm not saying that, Ben. Sometimes, keepers expect you to shoot to the far side. They lean that way, give you space at the near post. That's why it's best to take a look."

Coach reached into his backpack and pulled out his clipboard. "It's time to reveal the two activities you chose for New York. On Saturday, we'll do your top pick, a boat cruise around Manhattan. On Sunday, we'll go to a Yankee game."

Max pumped a fist. *My top two choices!*

Coach eyed his clipboard. "Okay, two more fun facts about New York. Anyone know who Betty Lou Oliver was?"

Fivehead raised a hand. "Isn't she the Who from Whoville in, 'The Grinch Who Stole Christmas?'"

"Funny, Wes," Coach said. "Here's a hint. She's in the Guinness Book of World Records."

With that, Ben stuck up a hand. "Did this Betty Lou fall seventy-five floors in an elevator?" he asked.

Coach's eyes lit up. "Ice cream for Ben! In nineteen forty-five, a plane crashed into the seventy-ninth floor of the Empire State Building. Betty Lou was operating the elevator. And Ben, you left out the best part. She survived, making it the longest survived fall ever in an elevator."

Fivehead put up a hand. "Coach, you really floored me with that one."

Coach nodded at Fivehead, and then he eyed his notes. "The next fact has to do with Central Park, the huge park in the middle of Manhattan."

"Hey, I know that place," Fivehead shot in. "I'm a hot dog vendor there."

The boys roared. Coach went on. "Anybody know what a 'Nannarrup hoffmani' is?"

Fivehead scrunched up his face. "Coach, I think you need some water."

Coach put up a hand to quell the laughter. "That's the name of a centipede that you will find in only one place in the world, Central Park."

"How can that be?" Ben asked.

"Central Park is so big and so isolated from other green areas, it gave rise to a new species," Coach explained.

"Sounds like somebody made that up," Fivehead sniped.

Coach went on. "This centipede is less than half an inch long. Scientists found it about twenty years ago. It's funny, people think of

Manhattan as concrete, glass, and steel. But nature thrives there, too. Pretty cool, huh?"

Coach took a stack of papers off his clipboard. "This is our schedule for New York. Take two copies, give one to your parents."

"So, Coach, who do we play?" Ben asked.

"In the first three rounds, we face teams from England, Germany, and Canada."

"The Falcons are in the tournament, right?" Artie asked. When Max heard 'Falcons,' he felt his pulse tick up.

"The Falcons are in the other half of the bracket," Coach said. "If we play them, it would be in the championship game."

"Let's hope that doesn't happen," Artie said.

"Why's that?" Coach asked.

"Because they'd kill us," Artie whined.

Coach stared Artie down. "Boys, you got anything to say to Artie?"

"Stop hangin' out at the deli, Artie," Fivehead said. "You're full of baloney."

The boys howled.

Later that night, Max dropped on his bed and eyed the schedule for New York.

Friday	Arrive early evening
	Explore Central Park
Saturday	First game versus England, 8 a.m., Central Park (all games played there)
	Boat cruise, 11 a.m.
	Second game versus Germany, 4 p.m.
Sunday	Third game versus Canada, 8 a.m.
	Fourth game versus France, 10 a.m.
	Yankee Stadium, 1 p.m.
	Championship game, 6 p.m.
	Return home

Max dropped the schedule into his carpet. *Can't wait for New York. It'll be a blast, even if we have to play the Falcons.*

The next morning, Max fetched the paper off the porch and yanked out the sports section. Leafing through, a headline caught his eye.

FALCONS TO PLAY IN GLOBETROTTER SOCCER TOURNAMENT

Max read the story. The first eight paragraphs were all about the Falcons. Their "spotless" record of thirteen wins, no losses, and no ties. Their eleven shutouts. Their top scorer, with twenty-four goals, "local hero" Red Peters.

Local hero? Max shook his head. *That's a typo. It should say, "local zero."*

Max kept reading until he reached the last sentence. It read, *another team from Chelsea, the Thunder, will also play in the tournament.* That was it, one lousy sentence on the Thunder. Max folded the paper, stood, and lobbed it up. When it came down, he drove his right foot into it, the sheets shooting off in every direction.

Mr. Miles had walked in just as Max made contact. "Another story on the Falcons?" his dad asked.

"Yep," Max said as he put the paper back together. "I'm tired of reading about Red Peters and the Falcons."

"Maybe you'll play them in New York," Mr. Miles said.

Max nodded. "Half of me really wants to, Dad. But the other half, not so sure."

After breakfast on Friday, Max checked his suitcase one last time. *Knew I forgot something.* He ran up, grabbed his toothbrush, and ran back down. Max hugged his parents and bumped knuckles with Betsy. "Have fun in New York," Betsy said. "I hope you take down some birds."

Max nodded. "Thanks, and good luck in Maryland." Later that day, Mrs. Miles would drive Betsy to her tournament in Baltimore. Mr. Miles told Max that he would try to make the two-hour drive to New York to see Max play.

For Max, the rest of the day inched along like a glacier. When the last bell finally rang, he shot out of his seat like it was on fire. Max hustled to the school parking lot, where he gathered with his teammates, Coach Pepper, and a chaperone, the teacher, Mrs. Brewer. They boarded the bus that would take them seventy miles from Chelsea to New York City.

A short while later, the bus chugged across the Delaware River into New Jersey. Coach stood with a microphone in hand. "Okay, boys, time for your reports," he said. "I'll give you the 'mike,' and you present from your seat."

Coach got up and walked the mike to Max. "Max, you're a paleontologist, so I know you 'dug' deep," Coach cracked. "Let's see what you found."

Max smiled at Coach's pun, and then he began. "I'm a paleontologist at the Museum of

Natural History. I study fossils. Fossils are the remains of extinct animals, like teeth, bones, and shells, or even footprints."

Max checked his notes. "Most fossils are found in rocks. I'm like a detective. I use shovels, brushes, and drills to gather rocks that might contain fossils. Then I chip away at the rock to expose fossils. By studying fossils, I can learn about what the earth was like a long time ago."

Now Max was rolling, his nerves settled. "Some of the coolest fossils are found at the museum where I work. One is huge, the remains of a dinosaur called, the Edmontosaurus."

Fivehead broke in. "Can we just call him, 'Ed'?"

Max went on. "Sixty-five million years ago, this dinosaur took its last breath in Wyoming. In the year nineteen hundred and eight, fossil hunters found its remains in sand and clay. It is considered one of the greatest discoveries ever."

Max checked his card. "Another popular exhibit at the museum is the blue whale. It's made of fiberglass and is ninety-four feet long. That's the distance from a corner flag to the near post. The exhibit is based on a real blue whale that was found on a beach in South America. Kids hold sleepovers under the belly of the blue whale at the museum."

When Max finished, Coach led the cheers. "Max you really 'rocked' it," Fivehead cracked.

Coach handed the microphone to Fivehead. With his other hand, Fivehead reached in his pocket, took out a plastic hot dog, and held it up.

"I'm a street vendor," Fivehead began. "I sell hot dogs, peanuts, pretzels, soda, and water. I got the best spot in New York City. My stand is near Fifth Avenue and Sixty-second Street, right next to the Central Park Zoo."

Fivehead checked his notes. "I sell so much stuff that each year I have to pay the city for a license," he said. "Guess how much that license costs me?"

"A thousand dollars?" Artie guessed.

"Hah!" Fivehead snapped. "Try three hundred thousand dollars. In the streets and parks around New York, there are a hundred and fifty vendors like me. There are four other vendors in Central Park that pay over two hundred thousand dollars for their licenses each year. Crazy, huh?"

Ben put up a hand. "How do they know how much to charge for each license?"

"They do it based on how much stuff you sell," Fivehead explained. "They let you keep a profit, but, man, they take a big bite out of your hot dog."

Ben looked at Coach. "Coach, I want to visit that vendor. We can count up the hot dogs he sells in five minutes, and then guess at his sales for the year."

"Good idea, Ben," Coach replied.

Fivehead finished, and then Ben went next. "I'm an architect. I design buildings and landmarks. One of the coolest landmarks we'll see this weekend is the Statue of Liberty in New York Harbor. She is known as, 'lady liberty.' The statue has broken chains at her feet. Those chains show the struggle for freedom in America and in France. America became a free nation in the year seventeen-seventy-six. Thirteen years later, France became a free nation."

Ben checked his notes. "Lady Liberty is holding a torch in her hand. The torch represents the values of liberty and enlightenment."

"Enlightenment?" repeated Fivehead.

"It means knowledge," Ben said.

"Of course it does," Fivehead yapped.

Ben went on. "The statue is wearing a crown with seven spikes on it. The spikes represent the seven seas and seven continents of the world. When we take the boat cruise, we'll ride near the statue."

Ben finished, and the boys kept going until everyone had done a report. By that time the bus was rolling through the Lincoln Tunnel, under the Hudson River, heading for Manhattan. Half way through the tunnel, the boys left New Jersey and entered New York. A while later, the driver pulled up in front of their hotel in midtown. Coach stood and faced the team. "You guys want to hit Central Park, maybe grab a hot dog?"

The boys roared their approval. After checking into their rooms, they met in the lobby. Coach and Mrs. Brewer led the boys on the three-block walk to the edge of the park. They walked north another two blocks until they reached the entrance to the zoo. Fivehead spotted the famous vendor, ten people bunched up at his cart. Coach and the players got in line.

Ben got out a notepad. He and Fivehead eased up next to the man and started to keep track of the orders.

Twenty minutes passed before all the boys got served. As Ben munched on a hot dog smothered in sauerkraut and relish, he checked his notes and did some quick math. "Wow, in thirty minutes that guy served twenty-four hot dogs. That means if he worked ten hours at that pace, he'd sell four hundred and eighty hot dogs. That's over three thousand hot dogs a week, or more than one hundred and fifty thousand in a year."

"Okay, Ben," Fivehead said, "stop showing off."

"I'm not done," Ben went on. "Each hot dog costs two dollars and fifty cents. Let's guess that each dog costs the vendor man fifty cents. That means he makes two dollars for every dog he sells. Multiply that by a hundred and fifty thousand, and he pays for his license with his hot dog sales alone."

Coach stuck a raised thumb at Ben. "You're a whiz, Ben."

"It's not fair," Fivehead whined. "Ben has a calculator in his brain."

Coach went back to the vendor and bought ice cream for each boy. Max and Ben each got an extra scoop. Back in his room a bit later, Max saw a new email message. He checked it. *Hey Max, good luck this weekend. I hope I get to see you on the field Sunday! Coach Ball.*

Max smiled. *I hope so, too, Coach. Sorta.*

CHAPTER 11

SETTING UP A SHOWDOWN

MAX WOKE THE NEXT MORNING, his eyes resting on a wall of brown bricks between the gap in his curtains. *Hey, where am I?* He rolled over and saw Fivehead sacked out in the bed opposite him. *Oh yeah, I'm in New York City.*

A bit later, the team met in the hall and rode the elevator down to the restaurant. Max ordered a bowl of cereal and a banana. When the banana came, he held it up to Fivehead. "Check out the brown spots, Fiver. This banana would make for a good smoothie."

Fivehead nodded. "You had a word for those spots, Max. What was it?"

Max thought for a second. "Flecks."

"I like 'spots' better," Fivehead said. "I can remember 'spots.'"

After breakfast, the players changed into their gear and then gathered in a corner of the hotel lobby. Coach paced. "Boys, we've had a tough spring season, but we can end it on a high note. Let's take it to these lads from Europe, deal?"

"Deal!" the boys shouted.

Coach led the boys on the short walk from the hotel to Central Park. As they neared the field, they passed the zoo. Fivehead spotted the vendor they had visited. He ran over to the vendor's cart and then jogged back.

"What was that about?" Coach asked.

Fivehead smiled. "For good luck, I rubbed my hot dog stand."

The sun broke through as the boys reached the field. After warm-ups the ref called for captains, and Max jogged out. The boy from England stuck out his hand. "Good luck, mate," he said. Max nodded. *Man, he has a weird accent. And he called me, 'Mate.' Never heard that before.*

Minutes later Max took the field, bouncing on his cleats. *These guys don't know me. I gotta strike early.* Twenty seconds into the match, Max gathered a loose ball in the circle and wheeled into open space on the flank. Sensing a defender closing in, Max lofted the ball into the corner ahead of Fivehead. As Fivehead ran it down, Max cut toward the box. Fivehead played the ball into his path. Max touched into space near the arc and cocked his leg, drawing his foe into a slide. But then Max cut the ball behind his planted foot and into open space.

Max took a quick glimpse at goal. Seeing the keeper edging off his line, he chipped toward the far corner. The keeper scrambled back and leaped, but the ball looped over his hands and slipped under the bar. Max took off up the flank. Ben met him and leaped on his shoulders. Soon, Max was buried under a stack of teammates. *Like Coach said, I looked before I shot.*

A bit later, the England captain stole a pass in the circle and sprang into space. Artie challenged, but the boy swerved around him. Max chased, but the boy was fast. He pushed closer to goal and unloaded from thirty yards. Max could only watch as the ball whistled past a diving Theo and stabbed the far upper corner. Thunder 1, England 1.

The game wore on, neither side able to snap

the tie. When the ball rolled out of play, Max heard someone whistle, and he looked that way. *Dad made it! And he's holding up two fingers.*

The England keeper launched a goal kick. Ben rose up in the circle and headed the ball toward the flank. Max ran it down and built speed toward the corner. Scanning the pitch, he saw Fivehead racing for the back post. Max eluded a defender and drilled a cross that curled away from goal. Max saw Fivehead closing in. *Finish it, Fiver.* As a defender settled under the cross, Fivehead leaped over him and snapped his head into the ball. It sailed over the keeper, struck the far post, and caromed in.

Fivehead got up and sprinted toward Max. They bumped chests in mid-air and tumbled to the ground. "Great ball, Max!" Fivehead screamed.

"Better header!" Max answered.

Fivehead's goal gave the Thunder a 2-1 win.

It was almost noon when the boys gathered around Coach and Mrs. Brewer in the hotel lobby. They rode a bus across town and boarded a boat for a cruise around Manhattan. The haze had worn off, giving the boys a clear view across the Hudson River to New Jersey.

Soon the boat set sail, gliding past the Intrepid Museum, situated on the Intrepid aircraft carrier. Coach pointed at a small plane on the ship's deck. "That's the Concorde, the fastest jet in the world," he said. "Once, it flew from New York to London in under three hours."

"Okay, Coach, so how fast does it go?" Fivehead asked.

Coach put up his hands. "I'll have to get back to you on that."

"No ice cream for you, Coach," Fivehead sniped.

Ben was tapping away on his phone. "The Concorde can travel over thirteen hundred miles in an hour," he shared.

Fivehead looked at Ben. "Nice work, Ben. Coach owes you another scoop."

The boat sailed on toward the southern tip of Manhattan. Coach pointed at a building that rose way above the others. "That's the World Trade Center Tower," Coach said. "Remember, it's the tallest building in the United States."

Farther south in the New York Harbor, Max could see a green statue rising out of the river, the Statue of Liberty. The boat swung onto the East River, and then chugged under the

Brooklyn Bridge and the Williamsburg Bridge. "Boys, there are twenty bridges that feed into and out of Manhattan," Coach said. "Pretty amazing, since Manhattan is only four miles long."

The boat took the boys around the northern tip of Manhattan and then back to where they started. By three p.m., they were back at the hotel, where they changed into their uniforms. A bit later the boys set out for the park. Once again, Fivehead ran over and rubbed his favorite hot dog cart. He jogged back to the team. "You guys see that line? There must be thirty people in it. This vendor thing is lookin' good!"

Minutes later, Max jogged out to meet the captain of Germany's team. The boy didn't say a word. He just shook Max's hand, shook it hard, and stared into Max's eyes until he blinked.

Two minutes into the match, Fivehead got fouled inches outside the box. The German back line formed a wall to cover the near post, and the keeper took his spot near the far post. Max felt a breeze in his face. He stepped up and thumped the ball. It rose over the wall, hit the wind, and snuck under the bar. Max pumped a fist and tried to run, but he got sandwiched by Fivehead and Ben.

The Thunder's lead held up until a German player cracked a long shot that knuckled over Theo and caught the far corner. The match stayed even until the last minute, when the Thunder won a corner kick. Max ran to Fivehead. "I'll jog toward the near post but circle out to the back."

Fivehead lined up his kick. Max started his run and then did a quick u-turn. Fivehead launched a powerful serve. Max leaped and nodded at the ball. It looped over the keeper, ticked the bar, and bounced in the goalmouth. An alert Ben had followed the shot. He thrust out his boot and toed the ball over the line. The Thunder had rumbled again. They held on for another 2-1 win.

That night, the team had dinner at the ESPN Zone. Back at the hotel, they gathered around Coach in the lobby. "So far, so good, boys," Coach said. "Tomorrow morning, we play Canada and then France. If we win both, we qualify for the championship game tomorrow night."

"What's happening in the other bracket?" Artie asked.

"Who cares?" Coach said. "We only focus on what we can control, right?"

"Right," Fivehead said. "Tomorrow is gonna be awesome. We'll beat Canada and France, then we go to a Yankee game. And tomorrow night, we win the final and take home the trophy."

"Fiver, Fiver!" the boys chanted.

The next morning against Canada, there was no suspense. In the third minute, Max cracked the net from thirty yards. Five minutes later, Fivehead ran onto a feed from Max and lashed home. Ben and Artie pelted the net in the second half, giving the Thunder a 4-1 win.

As the team headed for a stretch of shade thrown off by a row of tall oaks, they walked past another game. Max recognized Red Peters, in his blue Falcons uniform. Max tried to look away, but his eyes didn't listen. Sure enough, he saw Red gather a loose ball, cut between two opponents, and lash a bullet into the corner. Max rapped a palm on his forehead. *You had to watch, didn't ya?*

Thirty minutes later, a light rain began to fall as the Thunder lined up against France.

Max looked up and let a few drops dot his face. *Most kids hate it when it rains, I love it. That gives me an edge.*

Five minutes into the game, the rain came harder. Max stole a pass thirty yards from the goal. A defender challenged, but Max swiveled around him. He looked up, saw that he was within range. *Grass is wet, keep it low.* Max unleashed, the ball flying six inches off the turf. He watched the keeper take one step and dive. The ball hit the ground three feet in front of the keeper, skipped over his hands, and punched the net. Thunder 1, France 0.

Ten minutes later, Ben volleyed a cross from Fivehead inches under the bar. Early in the second half, Max bashed in a rebound from ten yards. With twenty minutes to play, Coach replaced Max with another player. As Max jogged off, he swung his boot through the grass. He stepped over to Coach. "Why'd you take me out?" Max asked.

"We have this game won," Coach said. "I want you fresh for the championship game tonight."

Max started to argue, but caught himself. The Thunder won, 3-1.

Back at the hotel, the team gathered around Coach. "Get washed up, boys, and then we'll head to Yankee Stadium." An hour later, the boys met in the lobby. Coach spoke. "Okay, boys, we're taking the subway. Does anyone know how many people ride the New York subway each day?"

"A thousand?" Fivehead guessed.

Max had read about this. He tried to remember the number, but he wasn't sure he had it right. "Six million?" he guessed.

Coach smiled. "Max, you're gonna get sick of ice cream. Now here's another fun fact. The New York City subway system covers six hundred and sixty miles. That would stretch from here to Chicago!"

Fivehead put up a hand. "Coach, we'll miss our train."

"One more thing," Coach said. "The ballpark is cool because you enjoy it with all five of your senses - sight, sound, smell, taste, and touch. When we get back to the hotel, I want you to tell me how you experienced the game with each sense."

Fivehead rolled his eyes. "Coach, you're not

making any sense." Coach lunged at Fivehead but he slipped away.

The boys walked down the street and took the stairs into the subway. Coach bought cards, and the boys went through the turnstile and onto the platform. When an A train screeched to a stop, the boys hopped on. Half way to the ballpark, the subway rose onto elevated tracks above ground. A bit later the boys got off at the stop by the stadium. They followed Coach through a turnstile and kept going until they reached their seats twenty rows behind first base.

Coach took lunch orders, and he and Mrs. Brewer went to the concession stand. Max led the boys down to the edge of the field for a closer look at the players warming up. When they returned to their seats, Coach passed out hot dogs and peanuts. In the third inning, Yankee outfielder Aaron Judge fouled a ball high into the air. The wind blew it toward the boys. From his seat on the aisle, Fivehead stood and watched the ball land ten steps below. The ball bounced high and came down a few rows below him.

Fans scrambled for the ball. Fivehead saw it

roll under the chair by the aisle. He took two steps down and saw the man's hand, reaching under his seat. The man couldn't see the ball, but Fivehead could. He bent down and snatched it before the man's hand could land on it. Fivehead turned and held the ball for his teammates to see.

"No way!" Coach shouted. The boys broke into a cheer.

In the ninth inning, Judge crushed a game-winning home run for the Yankees, a moon shot that cleared the center field wall by forty feet. When the boys got back to the hotel, they gathered in the lobby.

"Okay boys, I want you to knock some 'sense' into me," Coach said. "Let's start with sight, what did you see that stood out to you?"

Max put up his hand. "I loved the base lines, so chalky white. They really stand out against the dirt."

"Good one!" Coach said. "How about sound?"

Ben put up a hand. "How about the 'crack' of the bat when Judge hit the home run in the ninth inning. I mean, the stadium was rockin', but you could still hear that, 'Whap!' So cool."

Coach nodded. "Good description, Ben. Okay, how about smell?"

Theo put up a hand. "I love the smell of the cut grass. Plus, you could smell the pine tar one guy was rubbing on his bat."

"Well done, Theo. Okay, what about taste?"

Fivehead's hand shot up. "I love the smell of fresh roasted peanuts."

Coach shot him a sideways look. "Wesley, that's smell, not taste."

Fivehead slapped his big forehead. "The peanuts tasted great, too."

Coach shook his head. "Okay, the last sense is touch."

Fivehead pulled the ball from his pocket and held it up. "When I touched this ball, I felt this bolt of joy."

Ben followed. "I got to shake a player's hand by the dugout. Dude had a huge hand, felt like I was putting on a catcher's mitt."

The boys chuckled at that. And then Fivehead asked the question on every boy's mind. "Okay, Coach, so who do we play tonight?"

"We play the Falcons," Coach said.

"I knew it," Artie griped.

"I'm glad," Max followed. "We can ground those birds."

"Max, Max, Max!" the boys roared.

Max felt his heart beat a little faster. *I'm about to play the biggest game of my life.*

CHAPTER 12

SHOWDOWN: THUNDER VERSUS FALCONS

AN HOUR LATER, THE BOYS gathered on the sidewalk outside the hotel. Fivehead clapped his hands, drawing all eyes to him. "You guys pumped?" he asked.

"So pumped!" Max bellowed. But no one else said a peep. Fivehead hopped on a bench. "Guys, who plays for the Falcons? That's right, Red Peters. He used to be our teammate, and then he tried to destroy us. Doesn't that fire you up?"

"Makes me want to crush Red," Ben snapped.

"I hope he challenges me in the air," Theo followed. "I can use my fists."

"Theo, Theo, Theo!" the boys chanted. Coach put up a hand. "Let's not get too loud, boys."

Fivehead waved at Coach. "Come on, Coach,

Red Peters quit on you. I know you want to beat him bad, real bad."

Coach nodded. "You're right, Wesley, I want this game. Now let's go get it." Coach marched off, and the boys fell in behind him. As they neared the park, the sun inched lower in the sky. Max turned to Fivehead. "You think the Falcons will double team me?"

"No way," Fivehead said. "They're way too cocky."

The boys entered the park by the zoo. They paused so Fivehead could run over and rub his favorite cart one last time. As they reached the field, Max looked around. At the far end he saw his Dad, sitting in a chair near the corner flag. *Dad drove all the way up here again. I gotta put on a show for him.*

Max dropped into his stretching routine. He kept his back to the Falcons, so he wouldn't be tempted to look. Minutes later the ref blew his whistle, and Coach Pepper called in the Thunder. "They're going to announce the starting lineups," Coach said. "When your name is called, run out ten yards and face the crowd."

The Falcons were introduced first. As each

player ran out, Max kept his eyes on his boots. Max was the first player called for the Thunder. He sprang out of the huddle and sprinted out. His eyes wandered to his dad. Mr. Miles nodded, and Max nodded back. Out of the corner of his eye, Max could see Coach Ball standing by the midfield stripe. Max put his eyes back on his boots.

When each player had been introduced, the ref blew his whistle. "Captains," he called. Max got to the ref first. He looked up and saw Red Peters jogging toward him. Red put out his hand. "How ya doin', Max?" Red asked.

Max shook. "I'm good," he grunted. *What's with Red? His voice sounds different, and he actually used it.* Max lost the flip and returned to the huddle. Coach spoke, but Max didn't hear. He was in his own world, bouncing on his toes. *This is your chance, Max.*

From the kickoff, the Falcons strung together five one-touch passes. Their left wing dribbled into the corner and launched a cross toward the far post. Artie settled under it, but Red jumped over him and headed the ball just over the bar. Artie hung his head. Max ran over and hung an arm on Artie. "We can do this, Artie."

Max jogged toward the circle for Theo's goal kick. He looked over his shoulder and saw only one player, a boy with a blond buzz cut, standing at his side. Theo blasted a high ball. Max jockeyed for it, leaped, and nodded the ball wide to Ben. As Ben collected the ball, Max took a quick look into the eyes of the player marking him. *Okay, Buzz Cut, let's see what you got.* Max bolted out wide and sprinted up the flank. Ben lofted a long ball toward the corner, right into Max's path.

As Max neared the ball he glanced back and saw Buzz Cut closing in. Max slowed at the ball and swung his leg back. Buzz Cut slid to block the cross, but it never came. Max cut the ball inside and then veered toward the corner of the box. When the center back swung over, Max curled a cross toward Fivehead at the back post. *Follow your cross,* Max thought as he bolted for the near post.

Fivehead leaped and got his head on the ball. It arced over the keeper. Max slowed to watch. The ball hit the post and bounced toward him. Max took two steps and swung his left boot into the ball. It flew low and straight - straight into the far corner.

Max felt his heart hammer on his shirt. He started to run, but then he thought, *don't be a showboat*. Max beelined to Fivehead. "Great feed, Fiver!" he blared. With his teammates gathered around him, Max spoke again. "Okay, guys, now we know we can do this!"

As Max reached the circle, he heard Red talking to Buzz Cut. "Like Coach said, you can't let him get the ball, Teddy," Red said. Teddy nodded. "I'll stay on him tight."

Max smiled to himself. *Not tight enough.*

From the kickoff, the Falcons moved it around like a pinball. With short, quick passes, they whipped the ball from the left side all the way to the right flank. The wing built speed toward the corner. When Ben challenged, the wing blew past him and broke free toward the box. "On him, Artie!" Max yelled. Artie slid out wide, and Red darted into space at the top of the box. Max left his man and chased after Red. The wing played a ball ahead of Red. Red ran on and cracked a shot, but Max slid and deflected it just wide.

Max called in his backs. "We gotta mark real tight," he said. "Don't give 'em any space to shoot."

As the half wore on, Max had his way with Buzz Cut. He beat him to loose balls, and beat him off the dribble with ease. Max made several long runs wide and launched promising serves, but the Falcon center back was quick on his feet and good in the air. He was first to each cross, and adept at heading or volleying them clear.

After another of Max's crosses got headed out, he decided to try something different. The next time he got the ball, he spun away from Buzz Cut in the circle and dribbled up the middle. A back stepped up, but Max danced around him. He was still thirty yards out, but he had a good angle. Max wound up and lashed his right boot into the ball. It flew like it was shot from a cannon. *Bonk!* The ball hit the bar and bounced over. Max dropped to his knees. *So close.*

"Stay on him, Teddy!" hollered Coach Ball.

As the half wore on, the Falcons looked to feed Red on every possession. Ben tried to stay with him, but Red was too quick and too skilled. On three straight possessions, Red carved a path up the middle and set up his wings for good chances. But Theo was on his game. He made a diving stop, deflected another shot off the post, and tipped a third zinger over the bar. As the Falcons set up for the corner kick, Max ran back to Theo and swatted his hip. "Great work, Theo, keep it up."

The corner kick curled toward the back post. Theo leaped and punched it out, but it bounced toward Red at the edge of the box. Red took one step and lashed a rocket. *Bonk!* The ball rattled the bar and rebounded all the way out of the box. Max raced for it, two Falcons closing from the other side. Max got there first and tapped the ball into the clear. He looked up and saw only one defender between him and the goal. To his right, he picked up Fivehead darting down the flank. When the defender ran at Max, he lofted a high ball ahead of Fivehead.

As Max ran past, the defender grabbed his shirt. Max swatted the arm away and built speed through the circle. Max looked up and saw the keeper and Fivehead racing for the ball. *Get there, Fiver!* Max said to himself as he chugged toward the box. The keeper slid for the ball, but Fivehead got his toe on it first, nudging it toward the end line.

"Now!" Max yelled. Fivehead looked up and cracked a low ball across the face of goal.

Max ran at full speed. He lunged, got his boot on the ball, and deflected it into the open goal. Thunder 2, Falcons 0. Max was exhausted. He stayed on the ground until Fivehead ran over and helped him up.

"Great hustle, Max!" Fivehead yelped. "We're up two, can you believe it?"

"I believe it."

A minute later, the ref blew his whistle for halftime. Max jogged off, took a long drink, and joined the huddle around Coach Pepper. "Great work, boys. But we're just lumping the ball out of the back," he said. "We need to keep it wide, keep it on the floor, build the attack pass by pass."

"It's not that easy, Coach," Artie said. "These guys are fast."

"I get that," Coach said. "But possession is key. If we can keep the ball, they have to chase. And when they chase, they get tired, got it?"

The boys nodded, then Theo spoke. "We're giving them too much room," he said. "I got some help from the posts and the bar, but I can't be lucky the whole game."

Coach nodded. "Theo's right, boys. They

get within range, you've got to shut down the shot."

Max could hear lots of chatter on the Falcons' bench. He edged closer and listened in.

"Coach, we've never been behind," one boy said, "and now we're behind by two."

Max watched as Coach Ball put up his hands. "Easy, boys. We controlled the ball, but the frame was our enemy. I know we'll come back."

Buzz Cut spoke. "That number seven kid is good, real good."

"Yeah, Max is killing us," Red agreed. "We gotta do something, Coach."

Coach Ball rubbed his chin. "Look, we haven't doubled up an opponent all year. But we've never faced a kid like number seven. Billy, I want you and Bart to double him."

Max turned away. *Red says I'm killing them, hah. But the second half is gonna be different.*

And it was. Max worked hard to get open, but Billy and Bart kept him caged in. Five minutes into the half Artie tried to feed Max in the circle, but Bart cut the ball off. Red broke for the box, and Bart drilled the ball into Red's path. Artie went for the tackle, but Red nicked the ball around him. Crossing the eighteen, Red unloaded, and Theo dove. The ball sizzled past his hands and clanked the post. Would the post be Theo's friend, or foe? The ball flew across the face of goal, hit the other post, and bounced in. Thunder 2, Falcons 1.

Max ran back and put his arms around Artie and Theo. "We're still ahead, guys. Remember, pass to feet!"

"I'm trying to feed you," Artie said, "but they got you bottled up."

"So, play it up the flanks for Fiver and Ben," Max replied. "I'll try to give them a target."

With Max hemmed in, the Falcons took control. They attacked in waves, but could not find the net. When yet another shot spooked the bar, Max looked at his Dad. Mr. Miles put up both hands. *We gotta hold on for ten more minutes.*

Theo's goal kick pinged around the circle before settling on Red's boot. Without looking, he thumped a precise ball ahead of his wing and took off for goal, Ben a few steps behind. The wing cracked a low ball toward the top of the box. Artie and Red chased it. Artie slid, but Red spooned the ball over him. From twenty yards, he cracked a bolt right at Theo. Theo thought he had it, but the ball knuckled over his hands and punched the net inches under the bar. Thunder 2, Falcons 2.

Max watched as Red turned and ran back up the field. *Wow, no celebration.* Max called over Fivehead. "On the kickoff, I'll lead you to the corner." Fivehead nodded.

Ben tapped to Max, and he floated the ball ahead of Fivehead. But Fivehead was out of gas. The back beat him to the ball and turned to look up the field. Max figured the boy would pass up the flank, and he broke that way. The back chipped toward his wing, but Max cut in and chested the ball into space. Bart neared, but Max slipped past. Billy challenged, and Max sliced around him.

Nearing the box, Max cocked his leg and swung into the ball. As he made contact, Red slid in. Red deflected Max's shot over the sideline, and Max tumbled over Red. Red got up and put out a hand. Max took it. Their eyes met, no words spoken.

As the clock ticked down, Max and Red took over. They took turns controlling the middle and setting up their forwards, but both defenses held firm. With three minutes left, the Falcons earned a corner kick. Theo leaped and punched it out. But once again, Red was in the right place at the right time. He latched onto Theo's clearance near the eighteen, sidestepped Artie, and unloaded. The ball whistled over Theo's head and stabbed the roof of the net. Falcons 3, Thunder 2.

As Max walked toward the circle, he looked over and saw his dad hold up one finger. *I got one last chance*. Max took the kickoff and pointed to the corner. "Go Fiver!" he yelled, pulling his leg back. When Billy and Bart both jumped, Max tucked the ball under them. Gathering speed, he saw Red angling toward him. Max waited until Red closed in, and then he slipped the ball between Red's boots. Max glanced up. *Keeper's off his line, here goes*.

From thirty yards, Max stubbed his foot under the ball. It flew up and over the keeper. Max watched as the keeper scrambled back. *Thunk!* The ball hit the bar, popped up, and came down in the keeper's hands. The keeper hurled a long ball to an open wing. Max was bent over and out of breath. He looked up. *We're in trouble*.

The wing burst up the flank, no one near him, and dribbled to the edge of the box. Theo charged at him, but the wing dribbled around him and drilled the ball into the open goal. Falcons 4, Thunder 2.

Max could barely make it back to the circle. He tapped to Fivehead, and the ref blew the final whistle. Max dropped to the ground and stared at the sky. He saw a hand, and then he saw Red's face. Red pulled Max up. "Great game, Max," Red said. "You gave us more trouble than any player all year."

Max felt his mouth hang open a bit. "Good game, Red," he said. "Man, you got a great team."

Max was the last player to reach the huddle. Coach sucked in a long breath and blew it out. "Boys, you just made an elite academy team quake in their boots. You made me proud. Let's shake hands."

Max stepped through the line. At the end, he came to Coach Ball. "You played a tremendous game, Max. You carved us up like no other player has."

Max smiled. "Thanks, Coach. You have a great team."

Coach Ball nodded toward an empty spot, and Max followed him. Coach set his eyes on Max's. "Look, one of my players is moving to

California," Coach said. "I have an open spot on my roster. I want you to fill it."

Max felt his heart race. "I don't know, Coach. I mean, you have so many good midfielders. Where would I play?"

"You can play wherever you want, Max." Coach put a hand on his shoulder. "Think it over. Let me know by next week, okay?"

Max looked over at his teammates, gathering their bags by the bench. *I'm tired of being trapped in a cage. Tired of barely touching the ball.* Max looked Coach Ball in the eye. "Coach, I've already made my decision. I'm ready to be a Falcon."

Coach Ball broke into a grin. "Max, that's awesome! I'll be in touch soon."

They shook again, and Coach Ball jogged off. Max saw his dad and trotted over to him.

"What was that about?" Mr. Miles asked.

"Coach Ball asked me to join the Falcons," Max said.

"What'd you say?"

"I said I'd do it."

Mr. Miles smiled. "Max, you made a lot of great moves today. I think that's the best one."

Max nodded. "Thanks, Dad. I've never felt so good after losing a game."

ACKNOWLEDGEMENTS

My parents, Bob and Dorothy Summers, took me to England at age six and introduced me to the greatest game on earth. Laurie Summers, my dear spouse, read countless drafts and kept a fire lit under me. My children, Kate, John, and Caroline, gave me valued editorial feedback. My brother, Rob, and his spouse, Corie, provided unrelenting encouragement. A special thanks to their two older daughters, Kaia Summers and Ruby Summers. Kaia and Ruby read the manuscript, shared what they liked, and told me where I could do better. As much as anyone, they made this book happen. Once again, I'm grateful to the crackerjack team at Streetlight Graphics.

ABOUT THE AUTHOR

Bill Summers is a soccer author, journalist, player, and coach. He is the author of the Max Miles Soccer Series, made up of *Clash of Cleats*, *Cracked Cleats*, and *Comeback Cleats* (coming soon). Summers has also written the Shannon Swift Soccer Series, featuring *Magic Boots*, *Scuffed Boots*, and *Buffed Boots* (coming soon). He is the author of the young-adult novel, *Red Card*. His book on coaching, *The Soccer Starter*, was published by McFarland & Company. As a parent, Summers coached boys' and girls' youth teams for over a decade. He was captain of the men's soccer team at Cornell University, where he earned his degree in Communication Arts.

To learn more, visit www.
billsummersbooks.com.

Coming soon...

COMEBACK CLEATS

HERE'S A SNEAK PREVIEW

Max Miles sat in his mom's car, his boots laced, his eyes on the sunlit soccer field. But Max wasn't going anywhere, not with his seat belt still on.

It was Max's first visit to Greenleaf Park, for his first practice with his new team. The Falcons, the best under-thirteen team in all of Pennsylvania. But Max couldn't move.

"Practice is about to start, Max," his mom said. "Time to go."

Max blew out a sigh. "I've never felt this nervous, Mom. I can feel my heart beat, I swear."

"Remember, Max, Coach Ball asked you to join the team," Mrs. Miles said. "Besides, when you played against these guys in New York, you were the best player."

"Yeah, and then I fell off my stupid bike and sprained my ankle," Max whined. "I haven't touched a ball in four weeks, haven't run at all. What if I mess up?"

"Coach Ball knows about your ankle. He knows you won't be at full strength."

"But what about Red Peters?" Max volleyed. "I already took his position once, and that didn't go so good. How's he gonna react when I do it again?"

"Red was nice to you in New York, Max."

"Yeah, but now I'm a threat to him," Max countered.

Max thought back to his first few days on his old travel team, the Thunder. He was the new kid in town. Red was the star, until Max beat him out at center midfield. But Red didn't step aside quietly. He went after Max in practice, went after him hard, cleats up. Then Red quit the Thunder and joined the rival Lightning. But he kept hounding Max, with his elbows and his mouth.

After the fall season ended, Coach Ball had asked Max to join the Falcons. When Max decided to stay on the Thunder, what did Coach Ball do? He picked Red instead. After the spring season ended, Coach Ball again asked Max to join the Falcons. This time, Max jumped at the offer.

Max tapped a fist on his thigh. "Mom, if Red flips out again, a flock of Falcons might gang up on me."

"Coach Ball will squash any nonsense," his mom said. "Now get moving, or you'll be late."

Max unbuckled his seat belt and got out. As he walked across the infield of a Little League diamond, he saw a pack of boys gathering by the soccer field a hundred yards away. One boy looked Max's way, and then the boy started jogging toward him. Seconds later, Red Peters eased up and put out his hand. Max shook it, and they swapped hellos.

"When I heard you were joining the team, I was so pumped," Red said with a smile.

"Uh, thanks," was all Max could muster.

A whistle rang out. "Let's jog," Red said, "if we're late, Coach Ball will make us do sprints."

Red stepped into a trot, Max matching his stride. "So Max, with you and me on the field, we're gonna break all the records," Red said.

Max nodded. *Yeah, but what will you do when I take your position?*

As Max and Red neared the huddle, Coach Ball broke into a grin. "Max Miles, great to see you!" he blared. Coach met Max with a handshake and a shoulder bump. "Boys, let's hear it for our new teammate."

The boys clapped, and Coach went on. "You remember Max. He scored two goals against us in the Big Apple Tournament."

"Yeah, and then we buried him in the second half," jabbed one boy. Max remembered him. Tall, blond buzz cut, mean eyes. *That's Teddy, the kid I owned in New York.*

Coach set his eyes on Teddy. "Don't forget, Teddy, we had to double-team him, and he still ran us ragged."

"Yeah, Teddy, Max gave us more trouble than any other player," Red added. "He's awesome. Trust me, I know."

Max looked at Red. *What's with Red Peters? It's like he's a different person. So far.* Coach Ball fished a bag out of his backpack and tossed it to Max. His uniform. Max looked it over and then stuck it in his bag.

"So, Max, how's your ankle?" Coach asked.

"Almost healed," Max said, "but I haven't worked out in four weeks."

"Don't worry, we'll ease you back in," Coach said. After some stretches, Coach set up some dribbling and passing drills. Right away, Max knew he had some rust to shake off. His dribbling felt clunky, his passes wandered off the mark. After the drills, Coach set up a scrimmage. He put Red at center mid for the white team, Max at center mid for the red team. As Max took the field, his heart pounded on his shirt. *This is your chance, Max, don't blow it.*

CPSIA information can be obtained
at www.ICGtesting.com
Printed in the USA
LVHW040054101120
671184LV00011B/2023

9 780999 897959